## WANTED: Someone Innocent

"FOR GOD'S SAKE, MRS. MUNSEN,
DO I LOOK LIKE A MURDERESS?"

Her reply silenced me and sent a thin, cold trickle through my heart. "You had so much to gain," she said flatly. "I hated her, too, but I'm not young and I'm not in love. Keep your head, keep quiet and keep him out of it. I'll help you."

With that she left me, and I crept slowly into my clothes, feeling cold and sick with apprehension. That calm assumption of my guilt was something I never had envisaged.

## LAST ACT

"MARGOT, COME HERE." HIS TONE STARTLED HER AND SENT HER OVER TO HIM.

"What is it?" she demanded, and he stepped back to show her.

The hands of the clock were slender and finely wrought but they were made of iron and were very strong. And yet someone had forced them out of the true, wrenching the pins and twisting the points. Inside, the pendulum lay flat in the case, its shaft broken in two.

She stood staring at the damage, the senseless spite of it sending the colour out of her face. In this house, where so much had been talked of mock violence, this example of the genuine thing was startling.

BANTAM BOOKS offers the finest in classic and modern English murder mysteries. Ask your bookseller for the books you have missed.

**Agatha Christie**

DEATH ON THE NILE
A HOLIDAY FOR MURDER
THE MOUSETRAP AND
  OTHER PLAYS
THE MYSTERIOUS AFFAIR
  AT STYLES
POIROT INVESTIGATES
POSTERN OF FATE
THE SECRET ADVERSARY
THE SEVEN DIALS MYSTERY
SLEEPING MURDER

**Catherine Aird**

LAST RESPECTS
A LATE PHOENIX
A MOST CONTAGIOUS GAME
SLIGHT MOURNING
SOME DIE ELOQUENT

**John Penn**

AN AD FOR MURDER
STAG DINNER DEATH

**Patricia Wentworth**

THE FINGERPRINT
THE LISTENING EYE
SHE CAME BACK

**Margery Allingham**

BLACK PLUMES
DANCERS IN MOURNING
DEATH OF A GHOST
FLOWERS FOR THE JUDGE
TETHER'S END
THE TIGER IN THE SMOKE

**Elizabeth Daly**

AND DANGEROUS TO KNOW
THE BOOK OF THE LION
HOUSE WITHOUT THE DOOR
NOTHING CAN RESCUE ME
SOMEWHERE IN THE HOUSE

**Jonathan Ross**

DEATH'S HEAD
DIMINISHED BY DEATH

# Margery Allingham

# DEADLY DUO

## WANTED: SOMEONE INNOCENT
## LAST ACT

BANTAM BOOKS
TORONTO · NEW YORK · LONDON · SYDNEY · AUCKLAND

DEADLY DUO

*A Bantam Book / published by arrangement with
Doubleday & Co., Inc.*

PRINTING HISTORY

*Doubleday edition published May 1949
A Detective Book Club Selection, 1949
Bantam edition / November 1985*

*Bantam Books are published by Bantam Books, Inc. Its trade-
mark, consisting of the words "Bantam Books" and the por-
trayal of a rooster, is Registered in U.S. Patent and Trademark
Office and in other countries. Marca Registrada. Bantam
Books, Inc., 666 Fifth Avenue, New York, New York 10103.*

PRINTED IN THE UNITED STATES OF AMERICA

O      0 9 8 7 6 5 4 3 2

# WANTED:
## Someone Innocent

I didn't blame my uncle. I don't think anyone could have done that. I said as much to my landlady, the vast Mrs. Austin, one night when she sat on my bed squashing my feet in a wide gesture of intimacy in the horrible little room at the top of her house in Pimlico.

Mrs. Austin was a Cockney and kind and emotional, as they are, those stalwart old women whom no one suspected of gallantry until they suddenly produced it like a flag, and she had been saying with unintentional brutality that it was a shame I wasn't one thing or the other, neither the young lady of wealth I'd been trained to be nor the go-getting milliner's apprentice I was doing my best to become. Thirty-five bob a week was not her idea of a living wage, she said, and I could not have agreed with her more; seven dollars, Sally would have called it. I put Sally out of my mind hastily. It didn't help to think of her when there was only Mrs. Austin to talk to.

The old woman shook her head at me, her festoon of chins sweeping the unfashionable choker of marble-size pearls she wore. "You wouldn't do no good making 'ats, dear, not if 'orses wore 'em," she said. I laughed at that, but in my heart I agreed with her. What was more serious, I was sickly aware that Madame Clothilde was beginning to get the same impression.

Her real name was Ethel Friedman, and she was the nearest thing to a black parrot in appearance, but she had given me a job when Uncle Grey died, and she had done it partly out of kindness to an ex-customer and only incidentally because she thought I might be able

3

to bring a few of the right kind of customer to her shop in Hanover Square.

At that time, a year ago, I had believed she was justified, but then I was nineteen, fresh from Totham Abbey School, inexperienced and sanguine. Now I was twenty, and completely disillusioned, of course.

Mrs. Austin harped on her theme. "Holidays abroad and then no money! Serve 'im right if you end on the streets," she persisted. "Fancy dying like that."

"Don't," I said, "please don't. You don't understand."

She snorted. I sat looking through her purple bosom at Uncle Grey as I remembered him, an aristocratic old man, whose linen was laundered meticulously, whose shoes were very narrow, whose hands were long and gracious, and who had a sweet smile and a prim mouth, which yet could say gently witty things.

He was a bachelor of a vanished school, and when my father and mother had disappeared together under the green waters in the *Queen Adelaide* disaster, a frightened nurse had presented herself to him on the steps of Prinny's Club, Pall Mall, with me, a white-faced seven-year-old, clinging to her hand. He simply had done what he could for us, as he must have for any other two ladies in distress. He paid the nurse her wages and wrote her a reference. He placed me in the care of Miss Evangeline Budd, the principal of Totham Abbey, "School for the Daughters of Gentlemen." The fees must have surprised him, but I fancy he was gratified that it was the best old-fashioned girls' school in the country.

Before the European disaster swallowed his investments, he used to take me abroad every year. We went everywhere and saw everything, and always he treated me as a grown-up young lady whom he was privileged to escort. He was always considerate and never affectionate. I thought of him as a cross between God and a Cook's man.

When everything was gone save a small annuity, he died. He wrote me no letter, but one of the club servants came to see me at the Abbey and brought me his Georgian-silver snuffbox and the signet ring with the square amethyst. An insurance policy covered Uncle Grey's debts, as well as his funeral.

My upbringing proved about as useful as the other things I'd been left. My education had been excellent, but only so far as it went. I could write a respectable hand, but I couldn't type; I could balance my dress allowance, but I couldn't keep accounts; I could play the piano, but I couldn't vamp a tune; I could welcome a duchess to a bazaar, but I couldn't sell her a hat. I had not even made any useful friends.

At school, Sally had sufficed me. We had been such tremendous buddies that neither of us had had much time for anyone else. She was a year older than I, and by the time I was job-hunting, she had gone home to the United States and was now with a hospital unit on the other side of the world. I could see her quite distinctly as I stared into Mrs. Austin's straining gown. Five feet of dynamite topped with dark red curls, dark eyes with all the gayety of her race in them, and a mouth that, with all its impudence, was also wise.

"You ought to get married, ducks," announced Mrs. Austin for the hundredth time. "Perhaps you'll pick up something on this outing tomorrow."

"It's not going to be that kind of party," I said, laughing. "My headmistress is retiring, and this is her farewell reception to her old girls."

"If you ask me, you're wasting your time," she said. "You look a picture these days, but it won't last. It's wonderful 'ow girls do go orf, working about in London. Now's your chance, when you do look something. Don't throw yourself away on schoolmistresses. I wonder you want to go."

I had been thinking that myself, although not for the same reason. I dreaded the reception. Sally wouldn't be there, and all it had to offer me was a lonely good-bye to the one place I'd ever known to be any sort of home. Once the Abbey had a different head, it would not seem like my old school any more. It was my last tie with a life that wasn't bounded by the shop and the attic bedroom, and I was going to see it break.

I would have refused the invitation if I had not been silly enough to mention it to Madame.

She jumped at it. "Now, that is an idea," she said, her black eyes snapping. "That's more like it. If your friends won't come here, you must take the business to them. You can have the whole day, and you can wear the grey Lejeune bonnet. I want that to be seen. When people remark on it, as they will, just tell them they can get a copy here in any color, and only eight guineas. It's very nice of me to trust you with it, Miss Brayton. It's worth twenty pounds."

I told her I'd rather not have the responsibility; it might rain or something.

"You sell half a dozen copies, and I don't care if it snows on it," she said.

Totham Abbey girls are the daughters of bishops and the duller peers, and fashion is not and never has been quite at home there. The Lejeune bonnet was one of those extravagances Paris thought up in a joyous hour; the chiffon rose on top finished it—and me, too, when I thought about it.

Finding me uncommunicative, Mrs. Austin heaved herself off my bed. "What you want," she dictated from the doorway, "is an 'usband, and when you find one, 'ang on to 'im." Then she switched out the light. "You go to sleep," she said, "and termorrer make up your mind to find a way out of all this 'ere. This isn't your style, and never will be. Good night. Don't read, ducks. I must get the 'lectric bill down. 'Appy dreams."

I turned over on my face. As I lay there, it occurred to me that part of what she said was true. I must get out of this if it wasn't going to get me down.

The reception was rather harder to endure than I had expected. To begin with, the Abbey was lovelier than I had thought. The Gothic tower over Big Hall was more graceful, the lawns were neater and more green, the flower beds brighter than I had dreamed. They all held out their arms, so to speak. It jolted me.

On the other hand, the Lejeune bonnet was just about as unsuitable as I had foretold. I met Bunch Howarth as I went up the drive, and I saw her heavy brows rise as she glanced at it. Bunch is the daughter of an Estate in the Shires, and although we never had been buddies at school, that had not been her fault. Sally and I had not had much time for her worthy solidity. She was thicker than ever now in faultless tweeds, and her unimpeachable velours made me feel as if I'd come out in something from the finale of a revue.

"So glad you could come," she declared.

"Oh, I thought I'd buzz down," I said. "I was always fond of old Budd, you know."

Her blank expression was excusable, for neither Sally nor I ever had been pets of the headmistress. She still irritated me.

"I don't say I had a crush on her," I said, dropping into the school vernacular. "Don't keep looking at my hat, you gump."

She giggled, in exactly the same way she used to in class, and I almost forgot I'd seen her engagement announced to one of the Perownes. "It's sweet," she said, "but it needs bridesmaids."

That was my chance to attempt to sell it, of course, and I saw it, but I couldn't take it. Instead I said, "You can be matron of honor, darling," and added, "Are we late or horribly early?"

"Late, or at least you are. I came out again to see the garden. Everyone who has ever been here seems to have turned up," Bunch announced. "That incredible woman, Rita Fayre, is the lion, or was when I came out. You knew her, didn't you? She was Rita Raven before she married Julian Fayre. A bit of a publicity hound, I should think."

Rita Raven. The name came back to me over what seemed to be an incredible number of years. I remembered a tall dark girl whose black-brown eyes were piercing and, to my infant mind, slightly terrifying. She had been an outstanding figure among the seniors in my first term.

"She left almost as soon as I came," I said. "I never spoke to her. She's about thirty now, is she?"

"About that. Fearfully modern and all that. I'm rather surprised Budd asked her. She may be terribly wealthy, but she's hardly Totham Abbey style, is she?"

"Isn't she?" I said doubtfully. "What's her line—sticky divorce?"

"Oh, no. Only she's a bit of a mystery, turning up to marry Fayre after being abroad for eight or nine years. She gives fantastic parties, I believe, and gets a lot of publicity for her painting, which is odd and rather filthy. I thought you'd know, being in London."

"She's escaped me," I said. "I don't do my homework on the picture papers as I should. I was always vague, you know." If this was not true, at least it had been my reputation at school, and perhaps I had fostered it a little, hoping, no doubt, that it might give me an interesting mistiness beside Sally's lovely bright color.

Bunch laughed. "I don't know about being vague, but you've suddenly grown absolutely beautiful," she said. "I hardly knew it was you, Gillian. You've come into flower or something."

I had no reply to that, but I was grateful for her clumsy praise, for we had just gone into the Hall, and everywhere I saw faces turned toward me; some had surprise on them, and some curiosity, and some the thing I most dreaded, pity.

I left Bunch then and pushed my way to Budd, who was standing on a ridiculous rostrum under the central arch, looking exactly like a bronze of a plump Victorian statesman in classic robes. Poor Budd, she always did drape herself for a party, as if Nature had not done it for her already. As we shook hands, she eyed the bonnet, and a wintry smile flickered over her lips. I knew her so well that I understood perfectly. She was assuming that

I had put it on to create a false impression of affluence and she wished to tell me she was not deceived. She set herself out to be gracious, but she was also very cautious.

I saw Rita Fayre immediately; one could hardly miss her. The crowd round her was far larger than the straggling group beneath Miss Budd's rostrum. I recognized her, but she was smaller than I had expected, and it took me some moments to realise that I had grown a little since I had seen her last. Her eyes were still piercing, but she was vivacious and unbelievably soignée in mink and the chunky jewelry then so much in fashion. She was not beautiful, exactly, but there was a forceful charm about her, and she betrayed an acute sophisticated intelligence, which was impressive. I could well believe that she was much publicised; she looked like a celebrity.

I did not go too close, because, of course, I did not know her. We never had spoken, and she hardly could have remembered me.

I was drifting away when Rowena Keith bobbed up before me. While we were talking, I noticed the chypre. A fur-clad arm slid over my shoulder, and I was pulled gently around.

"Darling!" said a deep, effusive voice. "Here you are at last. My lamb, how pretty you've grown."

Rita Fayre kissed me before I could speak, and Rowena strode hastily away.

I came out of the embrace a little dazed. My impression was that the celebrity had made a mistake. She was smiling at me affectionately. "I'm Gillian Brayton," I murmured at last.

"But of course you are," she agreed unexpectedly, and slid her arm into mine. "And I used to be Rita Raven. Doesn't it seem an age since we used to tear about here together? Do you remember those revolting bands of licorice we used to share on Sunday afternoons? My dear, I *am* glad to see you again."

There was nothing I could say; I hardly could object to her claiming friendship with me, of course. It was extraordinarily nice of her, if incomprehensible. As she chattered on, the illusion became complete. It sounded as if we had been in constant correspondence. There were times when even I wondered. We had a royal progress through the room, and I began to enjoy it. From being a Cinderella, I became at least an attendant on the fairy queen.

If she was determined not to let me go, I certainly made no effort to escape. At close quarters she was a trifle overpowering; her forceful personality was imperious, and she had a way of sweeping criticism aside with a ruthless highhandedness I never before had encountered. After half an hour or so, by which time I was completely dizzy, we reached the doors leading to the main entrance and the drive, and I prepared to take my leave. As I moved, her arm tightened on mine.

"Let's get out of here," she said abruptly. "We've got to talk. I'm giving you a lift to town, Gillie."

"It's awfully good of you," I began, "but——"

"Nonsense, dearest. It's a miracle you've turned up at last. I only came down today to find you, and we've got some serious talking to do. Come along."

She swept me on down the corridor, and I blinked at her. "What about?" I enquired blankly.

She laughed and hugged my arm. "Sweet, vague little Gillie," she said. "Just the same, only a thousand times prettier. Yet you've not really changed; you still look faraway and slightly puzzled by everything. I'm so relieved; I dreaded to think what a year alone in London might have done to you. How are all the boy friends?" The final question was thrown in casually, but she made it clear she expected an answer.

"There aren't any," I said, as the Rolls whispered over the gravel toward us.

Her eyes flickered as we got in, and I saw that she was pleased. I felt somehow that I'd told her a lot more than I'd intended. Her next remark concerned the bonnet. "It doesn't suit you," she said. "It's far too old,

for one thing. You must wear a sailor. Lejeune intended
that for someone over thirty."

My surprise amused her. "I saw it in his Paris collec-
tion," she said. "Clothilde made you wear it hoping for
orders, I suppose. She really ought to have known it
wasn't suitable."

She took my breath away and made me feel transpar-
ent as well as uninformed.

"Oh well, that's all finished," she said calmly, settling
back on the cushions. "You've had quite enough of
Clothilde. You're coming home with me now, do you
know that?"

I felt it was high time to get a grip on myself. The
whole afternoon had been too much like a daydream. "I
didn't," I said drily.

She glanced at me under her lashes, and her bright
lips smiled. "I'm telling you. We're going to drop into
your boardinghouse and pick up your things and drive
home right away. Don't argue with me, dearest. I've
made up my mind."

"But I've never heard of such a thing," I protested.
"You don't really know me and——"

"Gillian!"

"I mean, not very well."

"Rubbish, darling. We were buddies years and years
ago. I used to do your sums for you. Remember?"

I certainly did not, but I did see that this was no time
to argue the point. For that matter, I did not know how
she knew I lived in a boardinghouse unless she had
been making enquiries about me.

"Listen, Gillie," she said, dropping her hand on my
knee, "I want you to come. You'll be a tremendous help
to me. Don't let me down."

She made it all sound so absurd, when she put it like
that. I hardly liked to explain to her that I thought she
was crazy, and while I was hesitating, I became aware
that she was offering me a job.

"Three hundred pounds a year, Gillie, and of course
you'll live with us."

"But—but you could get a trained secretary for that."

"Of course I could, my lamb, but I don't want a trained secretary. I just need someone I can trust who will be a little sister to me—do the flowers and that sort of thing."

"At three hundred pounds a year?"

A fleeting cloud of anger passed over her face. It was very brief, but I was startled by its intensity. "Don't worry, sweetie," she said, smiling at me. "Just sit back and take what's coming to you. You'll love it, you know."

I was so astounded that I did just what she told me. To this day I don't know if it was she or the Rolls that argued more eloquently. After the afternoon's taste of nostalgic luxury, my life at Clothilde's seemed very sordid and unimportant.

It was Mrs. Austin who put in the only word of caution that dizzy afternoon.

While the car and Rita's coat were making a sensation in the dingy back street, Mrs. Austin snatched a word with me. "Ducks," she said, squeezing my hand in her vast, damp one, "I know it's not my business, but I must ask you—are you sure this is orl orl right?"

"Perfectly," I assured her lightheartedly. "It's absolutely marvelous. Mrs. Fayre's offered me a wonderful job. I'll come to see you next week."

Her coarse, kindly face did not alter. "Mind yer do," she said. "I'll be worrying. You do read of *such* things. I'd trust you anywhere, but oh, ducks, are you sure it's orl aboveboard?"

"It's perfectly all right," I assured her. "Mrs. Fayre and I were friends at school."

"Ow, why didn't yer say so?" Her relief was ludicrous. "Of course, if you was friends at school, that explains everything. Orf you go, and mind yer step."

It was not until I was back in the car that I recollected that Rita and I hardly had been friends at school; but by that time she was setting out to be so charming to me that a trivial misstatement like that seemed a matter less than nothing.

12

\*   \*   \*

I fell in love with the house as soon as I saw it. We came upon it suddenly when we turned toward the river at Richmond. It lay among lawns at the water's edge, a rosy rectangle of Georgian brick, with a sugar-loaf roof and two modern wings, and the lights in its tall windows welcomed us in the windy gloom.

I stepped under a canopied porch into a wide hall, which was cool and gracious and smelled faintly of wax polish and flowers. An elderly butler, a wisp of a man with close-cropped white hair, came to meet us and showed no flicker of surprise as the chauffeur followed with my suitcases. I might have been expected. It was the friendliest, happiest of homes, I should have said, had it not been for one little incident.

Rita paused to speak to the butler, and as she turned away, I caught a glimpse of his face. It was gone in a moment, but I saw it—a gleam of unmistakable venom in his old eyes. He looked as if he loathed her. It passed through my mind then, at the beginning, that there was probably a lot about Rita I had yet to discover.

"Leave everything. They'll see to it," she said, putting an arm round my shoulders. "We'll go and see who's in the studio, shall we? There's usually someone here about six. I adore people to drop in, don't you?" Still talking, she swept me down a wide passage to a door set under an archway at the end. It was partly open, and I heard voices and the clink of glasses as we approached.

"Oh, isn't this fun!" her arm tightened. "You're taking years off me, Gillie."

It was fun, of course, tremendous fun, and I glanced round curiously at a vast, panelled drawing room, which had been modernised and done over in grey and white, with brilliant colours coming from the canvases on the walls. There were about a dozen people present, but they looked a crowd to me. Sherry was in circulation, and there was a general cry of welcome as we appeared.

"Darlings, I'm exhausted!" Rita went in with a rush,

taking me too. "I've been back to school, and it's nearly killed me. Meet my adopted sister, everybody. Can't you just see us both in pigtails?"

"Just, but only if the child was in a pram." The man who spoke came over, with brimming glasses held out to us. He dropped a casual kiss on the cheek Rita raised to him, and smiled at me with ironical approval. I assumed him to be Julian Fayre, Rita's husband, until she corrected me.

"This is Ferdie, Gillie. Not a nice man. Don't trust him. We only put up with him because of his money. How much older than Gillie do I really look, Ferdie?"

He murmured something in her ear.

She pretended to be furious and appealed to me. "Darling, do I look like your mother? What a horrible person he is. Come along, I want to show you to someone much more intelligent."

We went on through the gathering, and the badinage continued all around us.

"Sweetly pretty, Rita. Wherever did you find her?" a woman called.

"Nize little girl," declared a rosy individual, who, I am certain, saw two of me.

Rita smiled at them all, but did not pause, leading me across the room to where, on an enormous leather couch, a man sat watching us. He got up as we approached and took both her hands, but his eyes were on me. I saw a plump, middle-aged foreigner, carefully, almost foppishly dressed, with a pale, heavy face and round brown eyes. He wore a small black imperial, which enhanced the fullness of his lips, and I disliked him on sight for his way of peering into one's eyes, which I found disconcerting. I did hope he was not the husband.

"Adorable lady," he said to Rita, revealing a high voice and a strong accent, "you look so tired. Come and sit here with old Henri." He was still looking at me, and I smiled politely.

Rita seated herself, drawing me down beside her. "Gillie, my angel, this is Dr. Phoebus, who thinks he is

14

the most brilliant man in London. That's so, isn't it, Henri?"

"Possibly, yes," he agreed affably. "I'm not quite sure yet. Maybe. She pulls my leg all the time," he added, settling himself so that I was between them. "I am only her entrepreneur, you understand. I merely present her. I am the easel, she is the picture. She is the genius. Did she tell you that?"

"I was beginning to guess it," I said.

He had a gently teasing way, which was not altogether unpleasant, but I still did not like him.

Rita was excited and, unless I imagined it, very eager to please. She launched at once into a description of the school party. She made it sound very amusing, and Phoebus sat nodding and smiling, but his eyes never left my face.

"And so you found this little one?" he said presently.

"At last. Wasn't I lucky? She was my only real friend at school, you know. The only one I remember, at any rate. She'll save my life here. Isn't she sweet, Henri?"

"Sweet?" he said. "Yes, and probably good. Charming. But not the hat—that is terrible. Why do you wear it, Miss Brayton? It does not suit you."

I stared at him, not because of his remark, but because he'd used my name. It had not been mentioned since we entered the house.

Rita was aware of it too. She put a hand over mine. "I've talked of you such a lot, Gillie," she said deliberately. "Henri's always hearing about my school days. It is a horrid hat, dear. Do take it off."

The direct request sidetracked me, and I removed the bonnet in embarrassment.

Phoebus took it from me at once and turned it round critically in his plump white hands. "Bad," he said; "it is not style, it is only fuss. I forbid you to wear it again. In fact, I forbid any woman to wear it. It is a monstrosity, isn't it?"

He got up as he spoke, and Rita began to laugh. I had no idea what he was going to do, and his move-

15

ment, when it came, took me by surprise. He went quietly to the blazing fire and put the hat on it. One moment it was in his hand in all its foolish coquetry, and the next it was blazing like a paper fire balloon; the flames swallowed the net and ribbons greedily, and the pink chiffon rose on the crown nodded as it blackened and died. I was frankly aghast. I hardly heard the crow of laughter that greeted the incident. I felt I was in a room full of lunatics.

"Hey," I said, jumping up, and the laughter echoed all over the room.

"My sweet," Rita said, hugging me, "don't. Don't look like that, my pet. You shall have twenty hats tomorrow. Henri, you brute, she's going to cry."

"Is she? I must see that." He came trotting back to look into my face again. "No. Not a tear. Of course not, she has too much taste."

"It's all right with me," I said, disengaging myself from the two of them, "if you'll do the explaining to Clothilde."

"Of course we will, darling." Rita was still laughing, still clutching me, and she began to irritate me.

They were both treating me as if I were a pretty puppy someone had brought in; but while he, I suspected, was uneasy under all his affectations, she was triumphant and overexcited about something. I was prepared to put up with anything within reason, but there was something going on that I was not following at all. It was very uncomfortable.

"What do you think of her, Henri?" she said presently. "Isn't she absolutely perfect for it?"

He looked at me gravely. There was no amusement in his face, only earnest appraisal. "Perfect," he said slowly. "You are a very remarkable woman, Rita."

"Am I?" She was laughing at him, and for the first time he looked at her directly, his eyes fixed on her dark, reckless face.

"Terrifyingly so," he said after a pause. And then he

shuddered; I saw the tremor run through him as he turned away.

Rita's hand closed tightly on my arm. "Go up to your room now, Gillie, will you? Ask a servant where it is. Do you mind?"

I said no, of course not, but she had startled me considerably. She had become very pale, and when she spoke to me, she did not meet my eyes.

When I left my bedroom, which was in the old part of the house and possessed a powder closet that had been transformed into a tiny, tiled bathroom, I did not go back to the studio. Everyone had gone out, for one thing.

Rita, looking superb in white moiré and diamonds, had come to my room just as I was unpacking the last of my possessions. She was in a fantastic hurry, she said, but she had to run in and explain, because it did seem such a shame on my first night. However, I mustn't mind one little bit, for she'd make it all up to me later, and it really would do me good to go to bed early and get some nice sleep, wouldn't it? They were all going off to a reception. We'd have a lovely talk in the morning, and meanwhile old Mrs. Munsen, the house-keeper, would find me something exciting to eat and— oh, I'd be all right, wouldn't I?

It was all I could do not to laugh at her. She had forgotten the difference between twenty and thirteen, I thought. Some of that may have been my fault. I was still wearing the junior-miss dresses I had had at school, and I was certainly childishly delighted to find myself again in the kind of background I'd had long ago.

The room was charming, very like the one I'd slept in at Mentone one year when Uncle Grey and I went visiting the noblesse down there. "Don't worry about me," I assured her. "I'm having a lovely time. I'll start work tomorrow."

She said I was the dearest thing, blew a kiss at me,

17

took her cloak from her maid, who had followed her to my room, and fled downstairs to Phoebus.

I dined alone and in state in a room that would have seated thirty people. The butler, whose name turned out to be Rudkin, waited on me, and after one tentative remark about the weather, which he snubbed, I gave up trying to be friendly. Evidently his dislike of Rita extended to her friends. It was a long meal, and I ate it in silence.

After the coffee he unbent sufficiently to pause beside my chair. "If you would prefer to sit in the smaller drawing room, miss, I will take you there now."

I thanked him, and we set out through the brightly lighted but utterly silent house. He opened a door at last.

"There are cigarettes on the fireside table, miss. When you wish to retire, if you would touch the bell, a maid will take you back to your room."

It was all very lonely and formal, rather like staying with a rich great-aunt who had forgotten one was coming.

This new room was like a great-aunt, too, but there was character here as well as formality, and I suspected Rudkin of softening toward me for him to trust me in it. It was a period gem, each piece chosen with knowledge and kept perfectly. There were little homely touches, too—side tables with caddies on them, and even a petit point frame with a half-worked panel on it, as though someone had just laid it down. The whole thing was most unlike Rita. That thought had been tapping on the door of my mind all through dinner. The servants themselves were rather unexpected, considered in conjunction with her; their smartness was very different from hers. It seemed odd to find the two opposing styles in the same house.

It was about half an hour, I suppose, before I ventured to go out into the garden. The glass doors were hidden behind long plum-coloured velvet curtains, and when I pulled them back, bright moonlight streamed in on me. The night was so clear that I almost could distinguish the chrysanthemums in the borders that ran down to the water's edge. I stepped out quietly and wandered among the formal grass plots, feeling utterly happy. I was desperately grateful to Rita, and not least for going off and leaving me to discover all this alone.

I explored the garden as thoroughly as I could by moonlight and then wandered back to the house. It really was a glorious place; there still were lights in most of the windows, and I could walk along on the grass path and see all the interiors spread out before me like old Dutch paintings. There were the kitchens, where the servants were at a meal, a cosy little room I took to be the housekeeper's, and another that might have been a library. Then there was a gap, and I turned a corner to the west side of the building, which was partially enclosed by a small walled garden of its own. I thought it was in darkness, at first, and had just decided to go back when I caught the gleam of a fire burning in a room that otherwise had no light. I went closer and peered in through a pair of French doors. It seemed to be a music room—at least, there was a baby grand standing on the polished boards, and I fancied I could see a cello case in a corner. It was impudence, of course, but I had to go in. It was a year since I'd seen a piano, and my hands itched to try that one. I thought that if I played softly I should not be heard from the kitchens.

The doors opened quietly, and I stepped in to warmth that was grateful after the autumn night. For a moment I stood hesitating, but there was no sound except the crackling of the fire, and I tiptoed over and sat down.

The moment my fingers found the keys I gave up worrying about anything. I sat there playing very softly for nearly an hour. I was abominably out of practice—it shocked me to find out how much—and I vowed to practise every day if I got the chance. I got down to some scales right away, in fact, and worked hard for quite a time. It was marvellous to be sitting there in the warm darkness, making music and forgetting everything else in the world. I had paused and was rubbing my fingers and wondering how long, if ever, before they got really supple again, when it happened.

A voice very close to me, less than three yards away, I suppose, said quietly, "Do you often burgle houses to play the piano?"

I screamed, or it would have been a scream if the sound had not been stifled into a gulp in my throat, and my hands fell on the keys, making a dreadful, frightened discord.

"Oh, I'm so sorry," I said breathlessly. "I didn't know anyone was here."

There was a long silence, and then someone laughed, very softly. That was too much for me. I pushed back the stool with a clatter and made a dive for the garden. I had my hand on the latch when a light shot up from a reading lamp behind the piano, and I saw the speaker.

He was sitting in a wing chair on the far side of the fireplace, hidden from me by the piano's tail. I never had seen anyone look either so ill or so forlorn. My alarm was swallowed up in concern for him, and I went slowly back into the room. He was quite young, older than I, but not a great deal. So much was obvious despite his weariness, which would have been alarming had he been ninety. He was desperately thin; his clothes hung on his bones as though they were on hangers. Yet it was a fine face, sensitive and intelligent, but very pale and tired.

He smiled at me, and it transformed him. His wide mouth curled up mischievously, and his dark eyes danced. "Don't go," he said. "I liked it. Honestly. Even the scales. Do you touch the modern stuff?"

I said I did not get on very well with the new French folk, and he nodded and went on talking music for some minutes. I got in another apology at last, but he waved it aside.

"Please don't," he said. "Come when you like. I wish

20

you'd sit down. I'm awfully sorry I can't get up, but it's one of my bad days."

It was shocking to hear the old man's phrase coming from such a young one. I felt very sorry for him. "It was dreadful of me," I said. "I came creeping in on you, and you're obviously very ill. Is there anything I can do?"

"I wish you could." His mouth twitched a little as if he were secretly amused. "However, it's only temporary, they tell me, thank God."

"But what happened? What is it?" I demanded. It was impossible to preserve any formality with him, and anyway, the situation had an unreal, dreamlike quality. I was so absurdly worried about him; he was not the sort of person ever to be ill.

"It's called 'multiple neuritis,' since it seems to worry you," he said, "and in my case it was caused by my—er—by my being left out in the rain. No end of rain."

"In the Far East?"

"Yes. Bullet through the thigh, and then—well, I got quite amazingly wet."

"How long before they got you to hospital?"

"Two weeks."

"Oh, dear," I ejaculated, and knew it was an idiotic thing to say.

He laughed like a boy, but there was tremendous underlying bitterness there, and I knew I was on dangerous ground.

"I'm so sorry," I said, and meant it.

"My dear child, don't take it to heart." He was still faintly amused, but not annoyed. "It gets better some days, vanishes almost, and then returns in full force just when I'm celebrating. It's trying, but it won't last forever. The doctors swear that. Besides, I know it myself—I am progressing slowly. Cheer up, it's my funeral. You're a baby, aren't you? I thought you were older when I heard you playing. Now I see you're only a kid. You ought to go on with that music."

"I'm twenty," I said.

"Really? I shouldn't have thought it. One foot in the grave, eh? When did you first take up burglary?"

"In youth," I said. "It was dreadful. I——"

"Be quiet!" His dark eyes, which were blue, I saw suddenly, a very, very dark blue, were apologetic. "I won't have excuses. You came, although you may not know it, in direct answer to prayer. I was sitting here, aching in every bone and wishing to God someone would come and play to me."

"Were you?"

"Yes," he said, and took my hand and squeezed it. There was nothing of what Miss Budd would have called a "liberty" in that gesture; it was just grateful and friendly and rather sweet. "Sit down and talk," he suggested, and I obeyed him.

It was very quiet and pleasant in the dimly lighted room; the fire glowed, and the air was still full of the music. I was just going to speak when the inner door opened and an old woman came in. I saw her before he did, and I caught the suspicion in her face and saw it turn to angry certainty as her glance fell on me.

I guessed she was the housekeeper, which was not very brilliant of me, as she had done her best to make herself look like one. She was tall and very spare, with a sharp red face, which made me think of a defeathered bird, and her clothes were exactly like Mrs. Noah's in the wooden ark I had as a baby. Her black dress hung straight from her chin to her toes, and a black velvet ribbon held in the loose skin at her neck. Her only ornament was a small gold watch, fastened to her flat bosom with a sensible gold pin. Her hair was scraped up to a bun, and her long red hands were folded at her waist. None of these details impressed me particularly at the time; I was aware only of her indignation.

The invalid turned his head. "Hello, Mary," he said affectionately. "Not time for bed yet, surely?"

"Not quite, sir." She had a gruff voice, which she softened for his benefit, and it was very apparent how fond she was of him.

22

"What is it?" he enquired.

She came right in then and stood between us. "I heard voices, sir. I thought it was you playing, and of course I wouldn't disturb you, but then I heard the young lady talking."

"And that's not allowed, is it?" He was teasing her, but very gently. "Mrs. Munsen has decided to be my nurse," he said to me, "and not for the first time, is it, Mary?"

She did not smile. Her narrow eyes flickered at him meaningly, and she said a most surprising thing. "I didn't know if you knew who the young lady was, sir."

With an effort he sat up and looked at her. I saw the glances that passed between them, her assurance and his surprise changing to bitterness and resignation.

"No," he said at last in a new flat voice, "no, I had no idea."

That was all, but all the friendliness, all the warmth, all the heartbreaking charm went out of him. The glance he gave me was cool and definitely contemptuous. "Good night," he said. "Mary will take you to your room."

I had no idea what had happened. I was dismayed, embarrassed, as well as bewildered. I thought perhaps he was not allowed to receive visitors.

"I'm so sorry," I said to the woman. "I caught sight of the piano through the window, and I——"

Her smile stopped me. Had she told me in so many words that I was wasting her time and mine, she could not have put it more plainly. "This way, miss, if you please," she said.

I glanced at the man, but he was not looking at me. His eyes were bent on the fire, and his wide mouth was thin and hard. I was taken from the room as if I were a naughty child. From the threshold I glanced back, but he was crouched over the fire.

In the corridor I tried to talk to Mrs. Munsen, but she ignored me. "This way, miss." She might have known no other words, and she led me firmly to my bedroom.

By the time I got there, however, I had recovered a little and I was angry. I swept her inside with me and managed to insert myself between her and the door. "Mrs. Munsen," I said, with all the firmness I could conjure, "as you know, I only arrived here this evening, and I do not know my way about yet. Who's that I've been talking to downstairs?"

Her eyes wavered, and she shut her mouth tightly until she saw that I was in earnest. "Let me pass, if you please, miss."

"Oh, nonsense," I said, laughing. "Surely you can tell me that."

To my amazement she turned on me; a flush spread over her bony face, making it terra cotta, and her narrow eyes snapped at me furiously. "As if you didn't know the master of the house. As if his—wife hadn't told you where to find him."

I cannot hope to reproduce the venom she put into that word "wife," but at the time it was the news that staggered me. He must have been at least five years younger than Rita.

"Rita's husband?" I said stupidly.

She brushed past me to the door and turned only when she had gained the handle. "You're very clever, miss," she said, "and I'm sure you know it, but let me tell you you're doing what no decent girl would think about. You can get me my notice if you like, and I dare say you can as things are, but I made up my mind I'd tell you that straight to your face when I saw you, and I have. Ashamed, that's what you ought to be. Good night."

Even so, she did not bang the door, but shut it with a gentle finality that was far more insulting. I was very angry but even more puzzled. I could think of several possible explanations, but none in any way likely. I was hurt, too; that bowed back and those thin shoulders were very clear in my mind. It was so late that there was nothing for me to do that night except go to bed, and I did that, and lay on such a mattress as Mrs. Austin never knew, staring into the darkness and wondering about other things, how Rita could go to any party on earth leaving such a man, sick and lonely, to the care of servants.

Before I went to sleep, I had half decided to turn the whole job in and go back to Clothilde. There was something altogether too painful about this house.

In the morning, while I was still trying to reconcile white organdie curtains sprigged with currant blossom with all I knew of Mrs. Austin, a maid I had not seen before arrived with my breakfast tray. As she set it on the bedside table, she said that Mrs. Fayre sent me her love and hoped I would be down in time to see the doctor.

I sat looking at her in mild astonishment, waiting for her to explain. As were all the other servants, save Rita's Austrian maid, Mitzi, she was on the oldish side. She was a stout, pleasant-faced woman who wore an old-fashioned uniform, her high white cap enhancing the plumpness and pinkness of her cheeks. She said nothing more, though, and was going out when I stopped her.

"You did say 'the doctor'?"

"Yes, miss."

"I'm not ill."

"No, miss." There was not the vestige of a smile on her lips, and her china-blue eyes were hostile.

I was back in the atmosphere of the night before immediately. I tried a direct attack and asked her her name.

"Lily, miss."

"Tell me, Lily, who is the doctor and when is he due?"

"It's Dr. Crupiner, miss, and he'll be here at a quarter to ten."

"Do you know why I'm to see him?"

"No, miss."

She went after that, and I was left to coffee and reflection. I thought I could understand the resentment old servants might feel toward a new member of the household who was neither one thing nor the other, but they seemed to me to be carrying it a little far. At any rate, Mrs. Munsen had no intention of starving me. My breakfast was the kind that should be eaten off solid mahogany after a suitable grace. I had about a quarter of it and then got up and bathed and dressed. It was all very luxurious.

By daylight the house was lovelier than ever. It had a cosy, mellow grace I had not met before, and the sun came in gaily at the tall windows and coaxed the polished wood to glow as if age had made it almost translucent. I saw no one in the hall, and thinking I should be less in anyone's way if I waited in the garden, I walked to the water's edge and remained there for some time.

I could see the short drive and the front door from where I stood, and when the doctor's car appeared, I was ready.

Dr. Crupiner's saloon car should have warned me of the man. It was one of those vehicles Sally said belonged to the period when people built cars like cathedrals— with prayer. It was vast and high off the ground and had, I swear, as much brass on it as a band. I arrived in the hall grinning at my thought, and the smile was still on my face when a door opened and Henri Phoebus came out. He was carrying gloves and a wide-brimmed hat and appeared to be on his way to the street. I was surprised to see him in the house so early, and may have shown it, for he put his head on one side and shook a plump white finger at me.

"I always call early on people who have been to my parties, just to prove that I, at any rate, have suffered no ill effects," he said. "How are you, Miss Brayton? Perhaps next time you will come too, eh?"

"That would be lovely," I murmured without enthusiasm, and then moved sharply so that it was the air he kissed an inch or two below my ear.

He stiffened, and I suppose he was annoyed, but to my surprise I saw his expression was startled, almost scared. "Ungracious infant," he said lightly and pattered off.

But I had seen that look, and for the first time I felt desperately uneasy. After all, what on earth could there be about me that should have frightened him?

Rudkin appeared at that moment. I saw him when I was half across the hall, and I was not at all sure where he had sprung from or if he had seen the incident. His face betrayed nothing, but his manner was perhaps a degree less chilly than before. "I was coming to find you, miss," he said. "Will you wait for the doctor in here, if you please?"

He took me to the small drawing room I had seen the night before. By daylight the soft plum colours were very lovely, and I remarked on them involuntarily.

The ghost of a sigh escaped him. "It's a very beautiful room, miss," he agreed softly. "The dear old mistress loved every inch of it. Sometimes when I come in here, I can almost fancy I see her sitting over there with her needlework. She embroidered all these chair backs— gros point, they call it. It's very beautiful work."

It was as though he suddenly had come alive, and I turned to him. "Was that Mr. Fayre's mother?"

"The Colonel's mother, yes, miss. A very wonderful lady. Very different from——" He checked himself hastily. "The doctor is upstairs with Madam now, miss. He'll be with you at any moment."

"The doctor is here, Rudkin. Good morning, Miss Brayton. Permit me to introduce myself. I am Dr. Crupiner." The booming from the doorway brought us both round, and a truly impressive figure stood before me, two fingers graciously outstretched. Dr. Crupiner was certainly eighty, and my first thought about him was that he ought to go on the stage. As he shook hands with me, he led me to the window, presumably to see me the better, and I looked up into a handsome, conceited old face whose faded eyes peered into mine. He was a little tottery, but still very sure of himself, with flowing silver hair and sleek, old-fashioned clothes. He wore a great deal of jewelry, by modern standards, and his four-in-hand cravat was fastened by a fine opal pin. "Ah," he said, producing a pair of pince-nez on a broad black ribbon. "Let me have a look at you."

My impression was that his first concern was to see how I was reacting to this elderly magnificence, and it seemed he was satisfied, for he indicated a chair midway across the room and, when I was safely installed on it, took up a position on the hearthrug, hands behind him, handsome head thrown back.

"Now," he began, "to be brief. Mrs. Fayre wishes me to interview you myself, and I must say I applaud her decision. One can hardly be too circumspect."

I had no idea what was coming and sat looking at him in fascinated silence.

"You know why you are being employed?"

"No, I'm afraid I don't. Rita told me I was to help her, to—er—to be a little sister to her, but——"

"A little sister. My very words." He seemed delighted. "I understood she had been more specific. However, perhaps she was leaving it to my judgment. After all, I might not have thought you suitable."

"For what?"

"For a very delicate task that calls for the utmost discretion. You look a sensible sort of girl."

"I try," I said, hoping that I sounded less stilted than I felt.

"Yes," he said. "Yes. Mrs. Fayre tells me she has known you from a child."

"She knew me when I was a child."

"Exactly. That is what I said," he snapped, the point escaping him. "My late brother, Dr. Albert Crupiner, with whom I was in partnership, had the honor to prescribe for the Fayre family for a great many years— forty-five, to be exact. He brought Colonel Julian Fayre

into the world and a few years ago attended poor old
Mrs. Fayre in her last illness. . . . I understand you have
no nursing experience."

"None at all."

"Never mind. What we need now is intelligence and
integrity—above all, integrity."

"Yes," I said dubiously.

"We want you to be a companion to a convalescent."

"A companion?"

He nodded. "Now, Miss Brayton, you may not know
that it sometimes happens that when a man has had a
serious illness following the hardships and—er—hazards
of war, a nervous condition is apt to arise."

"Nervous?"

"Exactly. In this condition, the patient is apt to show
a certain marked, if temporary antipathy toward those
very people he best loves. Toward his wife, in fact."

I began to understand, or at least I thought I did.
"You're talking about Rita's husband?"

"About Colonel Julian Fayre. He is a delightful fellow.
He was my brother's patient, of course, but I have
known him since he was a boy, and I'm very sorry to
see him now in such poor shape. Physically he's im-
proving, but he still has this unreasonable distrust of his
young wife and, indeed, of women in general. Your task
is to dispel that."

"How?" I demanded.

"Wait on him, talk to him, listen to him. But——"
He paused and his old eyes searched mine. "You will
see," he said distinctly, "that it is of paramount importance that you should be entirely loyal to the wife."

"Yes," I said. "Yes, I see."

He appeared relieved. "An intelligent girl," he
commented. "Mrs. Fayre is to be congratulated. We've
discussed this very thoroughly, of course, and I told her
to find a little sister. It seems that she has done so.
There is only one other point. Mrs. Fayre has just told
me that you were considered a little vague at school;

indeed, that was the only doubt that crossed her mind concerning your complete suitability."

I felt myself growing red. It seemed an extraordinary thing for Rita to have told him. After all, she never had known me properly at school. "I think a lot of that was affectation," I said bluntly.

"Oh, that was it, was it?" He smiled. "Then I don't think we need to consider it. If I may say so, you strike me as a remarkably acute young woman. Now, as to details——"

He went rambling on, repeating himself and emphasising the importance of my loyalty to Rita, a point self-evident to me, but also revealing that someone, and I wondered if it was Rita herself, had given the matter very careful thought. There was a plan of campaign. To break the ice I was to be allowed to make the invalid's evening coffee for him, and I was to be trusted to put his sedative into it. The doctor gave me the tablets with minute instructions. I was told how to approach him and what to say if he should criticise Rita. I did not like it altogether, but I could see their difficulty, and I was desperately sorry for Julian Fayre. I began to like the old doctor, too. He was atrociously conceited, and he was, I suspected, something of a fool, but he had a great admiration for Rita and was anxious to help Julian. I suggested diffidently that maybe the old servants were suffering from a spot of the same trouble.

The old man glanced at me sharply. "You're very shrewd," he said. "Yes, between ourselves, I have—ah—heard certain rumours that would confirm that. Of course the old folk were devoted to their first mistress; she was a very gracious lady. Well, Miss Brayton, I will leave you to do what you can. I shall call later in the week, but never hesitate to appeal to me for advice if you need it."

We parted fellow conspirators. I was full of a new importance. My task was not going to be easy, but I'd made up my mind to attempt it.

On the stair I passed Mitzi. She had one of her mistress's evening gowns, which she was taking down to be pressed. It was a lovely thing, a shaft of silver slashed with flame, and yet, as I looked at it, I felt very sorry for Rita.

All the same, despite the instructions, I was not permitted to see my patient; Mrs. Munsen attended to that. Whenever I enquired, the answer was always an excuse. Colonel Fayre was reading, Colonel Fayre was sleeping, Colonel Fayre did not wish to be disturbed. In the end, I took my difficulties to Rita.

She listened to me with half an ear and told me not to worry. I took it that she did not want to discuss her husband with me, and I sympathised with her. If she wanted to leave all that to the doctor, I was willing.

It occurred to me that I ought to speak to Madame Clothilde and make what apologies I could. To my relief, her voice softened when she heard mine.

"Gillian!" Her use of my Christian name was an innovation. "How sweet of you to ring me, dear. What? Angry? Don't be absurd, child. Mrs. Fayre rang me first thing this morning and explained. Of course I was only too pleased to release you to her, and she's sending me a check for the hat. What an awkward accident; it caught on fire, I hear? Do bring her in if you ever get a chance, and I say, dear, if ever you need a little model for yourself, just come right in and I'll fix you up."

There was no stopping her. When at last she let me go, I was convinced of two things. One was that Rita was far more prompt and efficient than she had led me to suppose, and the other, that if ever I left her, Clothilde, for one, never would forgive me. Whatever happened to me, I never could go back there.

I was in the studio, putting the finishing touches to some flowers that had been delivered, when the man Rita had introduced as Ferdie wandered in. He mixed himself a pink gin from the trolley Rudkin always wheeled in at six o'clock whether anyone was about or not, sat down, and watched me, his eyes idle and introspective. Apart from wishing him good evening, I did not speak.

"That's a damned shame, you know," he said finally, and waved his glass toward the two oval bookcases whose glazed doors were set into the panelling on either side of the fireplace. To complete the modern décor, the shelves had been filled with bottles and glasses instead of the books or china for which they had been intended. The effect was not altogether happy, rather like the wine department in a store. "That sort of thing's all right in a smaller place," he said. "In a room like this, it's cheap. Don't you think so?"

It was, of course, but I did not feel like discussing Rita's taste with a stranger, and I said something safe about the moulding's being interesting.

"It is," he said. "I like it. It's all the original stuff. Silly to try to make it look like a gin palace. Well, here goes. I shan't hang about if no one's coming. This place is like a perishing morgue now the invalid is installed. You ought to have been here three months ago when he was still in hospital. We had some parties then. Phew! I don't know how Rita got her menagerie of old servants to stay." He got up and lounged to the door. "It's spoiled the place," he said. "It used to be like a good country club, at any rate. Now it's like a night club with the receiver in. I've never met Fayre. I hear he's a dreadful wet."

I murmured that I thought he was a very sick man.

"Not so sick as I am," said Ferdie with feeling. "The place is getting me down."

I dined alone again, and it was occurring to me that I should have to do real battle with Mrs. Munsen if I was to perform my one specified task of the day and administer Colonel Fayre's sedative, when she appeared. She followed Rudkin into the room with the coffee and stood respectfully just inside the doorway. There were candles on the table, and as the light flickered on her face, I saw how much she resembled the old butler. The likeness was so pronounced that I stared at them.

"Are you brother and sister?" I asked.

The question startled her, and for an instant she was almost human. "Yes, miss. He's a little older than I am. We've been here sixty years between us."

"That's wonderful," I said, with honesty. "You must have seen a lot of changes."

I wanted to hear talk of the old Mrs. Fayre, who had caught my imagination, but as if she resented my intrusion, she froze again.

"If you please, miss, I've come to show you the pantry where you're to make the master's coffee."

I got up at once. This was more like it. I was going to have a little co-operation at last. She held out a key to me, and I looked at it in surprise.

"Does it have to be locked?"

"Mrs. Fayre gave orders. You're to have the key so that we—so that no one interferes."

Her face was stony, and I sympathised with her indignation. "I'm sure she didn't mean you to take it quite like that, Mrs. Munsen," I said. "If you've been here thirty years, you must know best how things ought to be done."

It was flagrant soft-soaping, and she was not blandished by it; her small black eyes were contemptuous. "Perhaps you'll follow me, miss," she said.

I did what I was told. I had the bottle of tablets the doctor had given me. It was a small yellow phial of the familiar kind and was labelled carefully in just the spiky, old-fashioned hand one would have expected of Dr. Crupiner. To placate the old woman I showed it to her, and she unbent sufficiently to read the directions aloud. *"Colonel Julian Fayre. Four to be taken in a warm drink an hour before bedtime."*

"Perhaps you'd do it tonight," I said. "I'll watch you."

She nodded agreement, but her lips were set tight and her eyes were still contemptuous. If I was going to

make any headway here at all, it was going to take time.
I decided to go carefully.

It was on the fifth evening that I made my appeal to
her. We were in the pantry after yet another lonely
dinner, for Rita never seemed to be in the house unless
there was a party on. I was making the coffee.

The pantry was a charming affair and had been, I
suspected, the original stillroom. Now it was all apple-
green paint and antique spice cupboards; the china was
Victorian with a thousand tiny rosebuds scattered over
its duck's-egg glaze.

Mrs. Munsen and I had fallen into a curious arrangement. Although the place was technically mine and I
certainly kept the key, she always came with me when I
went into it. She collected me about a quarter to nine,
and we went into it together; then she stood back while
I took down the green-and-gold tin of coffee. It was
called "Kaffir," I remember, and had a picture of a
native on the lid. She watched while I boiled the milk
and counted the tablets into the steaming cup. Then I
carried the tray, a little yellow one from the rack above
the cupboard, and we processioned down the corridor
to the music room. She knocked and I entered, and she
waited outside until Julian Fayre had thanked me gravely
and I had come out again. It was a fantastic waste of
time, of course, but that seemed about as far as I was
going to get. Rita was being obeyed to the letter, but
that was all.

Every day I made some attempt to do a little more,
but with no result. Once I took the bull by the horns
and went to the music room uninvited. Julian Fayre
was polite but very cold and very definite, and the
half-amused, half-pitying smile he gave me was very
hard to bear.

On that fifth evening, therefore, after I had lighted
the spirit stove, I turned to the housekeeper. "Mrs.
Munsen," I began cautiously, "why do you imagine I
am here?"

To my amazement she blushed. "I should have thought

34

you'd have known that far better than I do, miss," she said.

Although I did not understand the inference, it was obvious that it was unpleasant, and my smouldering anger suddenly took fire. I am not naturally loquacious, but on this occasion I was at least expressive. I retailed the entire story, finishing with the doctor's instructions.

"There!" I said, pink and breathless. "Those are the simple facts. I have been brought into this house solely because I am a person who can be trusted. Why do you persist in treating me as if that were the one thing I am not?"

I could see that I had shaken her. She dropped some of her hostility; she was very curious. "Is that all you were told, miss?" Her eyes held mine as if they would draw the truth out of me.

I met her openly enough. After all, I had nothing to hide. "That's all," I said. "So there's no mysterious danger in me, is there?"

She did not answer that, but after a pause she said slowly, "It's a funny thing, but only yesterday Rudkin said he didn't believe you knew what you were doing."

"What?"

"Nothing, miss. I shouldn't have spoken."

I could get no more out of her, and that evening our nightly ritual was repeated in every detail; but she must have spoken to her master, for the next day he sent for me. I played to him for an hour, and afterward we had tea together.

That was the beginning; but the task was not over; the ice was still pretty thick. I worked hard and watched my step all the time.

If Julian wanted to talk, I listened; if he wanted a book, I found it, and in my spare time read it myself in case he should care to discuss it. I tried hard to discover anything that might interest him, and I took Mrs. Munsen into my confidence at every point.

Very soon I forgot it was part of the job and began to

enjoy it. Any improvement he showed gave me genuine delight, and on his bad days I was as disappointed as he. All the same, our relationship was still oddly impersonal. He treated me as a child treats a visiting governess, with politeness but no familiarity, and I was careful not to demand any more. This went on for about a fortnight, I suppose, during which time the servants grew less unfriendly, Rita hardly appeared, and the doctor was encouraging. The change came one afternoon. I had gone to him with the evening papers. Like most men who have been overseas for any length of time, he had a morbid conviction that he was out of touch with the ordinary happenings of the day, and we were correcting that by a study of the news far more thorough than necessary. That day the Education Bill was in the headlines, and he began to talk of schools.

"I knew a charming old man with the same name as yours once," he said, looking at me. "I always remember him because he once came to the station with my father to see me off, and he gave me a sovereign—not a note, but gold. He had a queer name, Grey Brayton. Ever heard of him?"

"Uncle Grey," I said, and after that no one could have kept me quiet. It was so long since I had had anyone to talk to that I chattered on about the old man until all my loneliness and regret for his death seemed to escape and become dispersed in the flood of words.

"My hat, you adored him, didn't you?" Julian said. "I didn't realize you were his niece."

"I loved him," I said. "He was the only family I had, you see."

He raised his head at that, and there was startled enquiry in his eyes. "Do you mean to say you have no one who belongs to you, no one at all?"

"No," I said cheerfully. "If I die tomorrow, there's no one to write to—except Sally, perhaps."

"Sally?"

I was only too pleased to talk; he heard all about

36

Sally, and after that, for good measure, even about Mrs. Austin and Madame Clothilde.

When I had finished, he said an odd thing. "You're completely alone, aren't you? Is that why my wife picked on you, I wonder?"

"I don't think so," I put in quickly. "I think she just did it out of kindness. She knew me at school."

He made no comment on that, but still eyed me curiously, as if a new and worrying idea had occurred to him. It was the first time I ever had heard him speak of Rita, and as far as I knew, he had not seen her since I had been in the house. Although they lived under the same roof, their lives hardly could have been more separate. He did not pursue the subject, however, and when he spoke again, it was about his own childhood.

After that we had many talks; our lives grew imperceptibly closer. I never had been happier, and his health began to improve. The bad days became more and more infrequent, and Dr. Crupiner was delighted. I saw less and less of Rita; if she was busy, so was I, and although we smiled at each other as we passed in the hall and met sometimes at the dinner table, there were always guests, and I don't think I had a single talk with her.

Henri Phoebus lived quite near us, I discovered. He always was dropping in, and his exertions as Rita's entrepreneur appeared to be considerable. She was going to have an exhibition of her paintings, he told me once, and he was up to his eyes in work preparing for it. But although I saw him fairly often, he never made another pass at me, and I always got the impression that he was slightly uncomfortable in my presence, as if I frightened him a little, which was ridiculous. So far as I knew, Julian had no idea of his existence. I did not enlighten him.

One night when I was sitting with Julian after dinner, before it was time to make the Kaffir, he began to talk about his mother, and after that the house became twice as real to me. It was hers, of course; only the studio reflected Rita's taste. The rest was just as old Mrs. Fayre had left it, and from Julian's description I began to fancy I could see her about the house almost as clearly as old Rudkin did. She had been a straight-backed, handsome old lady, with a firm voice and a smile that must have been like Julian's, sudden and oddly sweet. He had adored her. He did not say so, but it was apparent in every word he spoke, and when he mentioned her death, his face grew grim.

"She died in such pain," he said savagely, as if the justice of that cruelty still rankled with him, "the year before I went overseas."

"Only a year? Then she must have known Rita."

"No." He was frowning, and he looked so bitter I wished I had not spoken. "No, I met my—wife two months before I sailed."

So that was how it had happened. I often had specu-lated; now it seemed clear to me that there had been one of those violent love affairs that were so common in the catastrophic years, love affairs that all too often had this kind of ending. I thought I understood all about it, and I was tremendously sorry for both of them. To change the subject, I remarked that Mrs. Munsen had told me she had been in the house for thirty years.

"Mary?" he said. "Good Lord, no. She's lying; it must be nearer fifty. She's getting skittish about her age. Her husband was the gardener here, and he died before I was born. She nursed me when I was in long clothes."

"She's a wonderful old person," I said.

"Isn't she?" he agreed. "But the great character was Harriet, mother's personal maid. You really ought to have seen her, Gillie. She married Rudkin just to keep him in the family, or so my father always said. She was a terrific old party, and she lived for Mother. They were the same age, and she died only six weeks after Mother did. When she went, too, and I had to go abroad, I had no idea what to do with everyone. It worried the life out of me."

I caught a glimpse then of something that had not occurred to me before. I never had thought that a house like this with a company of old servants like Mary and Lily and Rudkin might be almost as much of a responsibility as a family. I was going to say so when his next remark diverted me.

"Have you ever heard Mary sing?"

"Sing?" I echoed, laughing.

He nodded, his face lighting up with pure mischief. "Rather rude old music-hall songs. She used to sing them to me when I was a child, and my mother was scandalised. We'll get her in here one night and make her do it again, shall we?"

We did. A few days later, when everyone else was safely out, Julian and I got old Mrs. Munsen in her black frock, with her little watch shaking on her chest, sitting back in a big chair and bellowing, "The captain with his whiskers gave a sly glance at me," in a surprisingly strong, if cracked, old country voice.

She betrayed a merriness I had not dreamed was in her, and she giggled like a girl when Julian teased her. It was an innocent but genuinely uproarious evening, and we all laughed until the tears streamed down our cheeks.

I saw him that night for the first time, I think; at least, that was when I first recognised him for what he was, not a burnt-out war hero, but a young man happy and heartbreakingly handsome, with a life before him. I went to bed feeling oddly breathless, but joyful and excited. He was really getting well at last, and it was I who was doing it.

After that, I suppose, the end was inevitable; yet I did not see it coming, and when it happened, it descended on me with all the cruelty of surprise.

I had been there nine weeks and three days. It was on a real midwinter afternoon, when there was snow on the lawns and slush in the roads, the air crisp, and indoors the fires burning brightly. In the morning I had been more than happy. Life had achieved that state of overpacked goodness that is delight. Rita had let me know that she was pleased with me, the servants smiled on me whenever they saw me, and Dr. Crupiner had startled himself even more than he had me by actually patting me on the head in an excess of professional approval. Julian was better; his weight was beginning to go up, and he was alive and interested.

That afternoon he was in the library with Mr. Churchman, his attorney who managed his affairs. I was waiting tea for them in the music room, where we spent most of the time, because it was quiet and away from the rest of the house.

I had turned up the lights and drawn the curtains, and the fire was blazing. My only concern in the world at that moment was to prevent the pup's getting the scones. He was a recent acquisition. Rita loathed animals, and we had to keep the dog, if not a secret, at least at the stage of circumstantial rumour. He was a bull terrier, three months old, fat as butter, with a couple of patches in the right places, and his name was Stinker. We changed it to Tinker in polite society, but when we were alone, Stinker it was.

He was fighting me for the scones and behaving abominably; his great plump paws were scratching my neck while he made unsuccessful dabs at my face with an urgent pink tongue. I was laughing and pushing him down when we both, the dog and I, were aware that Julian had come in. He stood in the doorway looking at us, and there was something in his eyes I never had seen before. Stinker went thumping over to him, bouncing round with his flurried-kitten technique, which was so funny in such a fat dog; but for once he was ignored.

Julian shut the door and came over to me. He was still looking at me in the new, odd way, which I longed and yet dreaded to see.

"Churchman couldn't stay," he said, and hesitated.

"Come and sit down," I said hastily. "You'll tire yourself with business, and that's just plain crazy when you're getting well. Don't worry about anything. If you go broke, Mrs. Munsen and I will take up charring. Stinker would be invaluable as a washing-up machine, if no one took mustard."

I was talking disjointed rubbish because I wanted time. I had seen that the thing I had thrust far out of my mind was going to happen, not in some faraway nebulous future, but now, this instant. I wanted it to happen so badly that I could scarcely breathe, but I knew it was the one thing that never must happen if I was to hold one shred of my present happiness.

"Hold the animal while I pour," I said.

"All right."

He seized Stinker in mid-air and sat down with him, but I knew I had only postponed it. When it came, it was far worse, yet much better than I had dreamed, because he had faced it and been wise.

"Gillie," he said, regarding me steadily, his thin face very grave, "I'm afraid you've got to leave here, my dear, d'you know."

I met his eyes. It was no good funking it. After that there was no need for him to tell me any more.

The room smelled of flowers and the fresh, sweet scent of tea, and because we were so quiet, the faint sound of the traffic reached us from the road. I was miserable, yet behind it all recklessly and fiercely happy. At that moment it was worth a lifetime's banishment to know the thing that only his eyes had told me.

"I've known for a long time that this would have to happen," he said, "and I've been putting it away from me, because I can't think how I'm going to get on without you, but just now, when I came in and saw you here, by my fire, with that damned presumptuous pup, I——"

"Look," I said quickly. "Don't. Don't say anything. Let me just go to Rita and say I'm leaving."

He was silent for a time, his eyes holding mine. "All right, Gillie," he said at last, and that was all.

I think I died a little just then.

Rita was out when I went to look for her, but I caught her at last in her dressing room. From the instant I left the music room I realised I should have to leave the house at once. There was dynamite in our association, Julian's and mine. Every hour of proximity meant pain for both of us, and although we were being resolutely intelligent, it was not easy. I did not trust myself.

I had some difficulty in getting in to see Rita. Mitzi was with her, and they were busy with clothes. The sable cloak was out, so I assumed she was off to yet another party. She was sitting at the dressing table curling her lashes; her eyes were fixed on her reflection, and the operation was a delicate one. She listened to my announcement without showing that she had heard. She did not answer for a moment, but finished turning the long black lashes upward and then laid down the instrument, its silver rim making a little impatient click on the plate glass.

"Darling Gillie," she sighed, turning and taking my hands. She was smiling as usual, but her deep voice had an edge to it. "I'm due down the road in seven minutes. Come and see me tomorrow, and we'll smooth away all your little troubles. You must be finding life incredibly dull here. I do know, my pet. But we'll change all that, Rita promises."

Dull! I could have laughed at her. She seemed suddenly so stupid sitting there, making up her mature, hard face for Henri Phoebus and his friends, when someone so tremendously worth while was being lost to her.

"I'm sorry," I said. "I know it's inconvenient, but I just wanted to tell you I'm going. I couldn't very well walk out without saying good-bye."

"But of course you're not going. I'm delighted with you, you're a success, Gillie."

"No, Rita," I said. "Please. I do mean it. Thank you tremendously, and good-bye."

I tried to sound convincing, and succeeded. The moment when the fact dawned on her was visible. Her friendliness vanished as if it had been discarded like a garment, and the angry colour spread up her face to the roots of her hair. Mitzi was sent out of the room with a gesture, and Rita turned on me.

"You hopeless little fool," she said. "What the hell's the matter now?"

I had made up my mind that it would be easier to give no explanation. It was a free country, and I was going. I was grateful, and I was sorry if I was being a nuisance, but it was no use talking to me. I would leave the house now, tonight; I felt it would be better that way, and I let her think what she would of me.

Rita got up. I had heard of viragoes but I never had met one before. She was so strong, so unexpectedly coarse under her sophistication, that I was startled and, I suppose, shocked. I began to understand what Julian must have discovered about her after he had married her.

"Now will you go to your room?" She was breathless, and there were ugly lines round her mouth. "I'll see you in the morning."

"No," I said. "I'm sorry you're taking it like this, Rita, but really I'm afraid there is nothing I can say. I——"

The rest of the sentence was lost, because she hit me. It was a savage flip across my face with the back of her hand. The pain was sharp and incredibly insulting, and I froze at it.

"Very well," I said, and turned away.

She sprang between me and the door, and behind her fury I was aware of something new. There was a calculating, dangerous mentality there, powerful and overwhelming. "You will stay."

"No, Rita."

"I see." She picked up the dress Mitzi had laid out for her and pitched it across the room. It was done almost quietly, with a new, controlled deliberation more alarming than her raging. "Go and pack. You can leave in the morning. I hope I never see you again."

It was on the tip of my tongue to insist that I should go at once, but I knew I had won my point and the extra night seemed to matter very little.

I had opened the door when she caught my wrist. She was trembling with something that was almost excitement, and now there was urgency rather than anger in her voice. "Tomorrow I shall get someone to take your place, but meanwhile I won't have the rhythm of the house upset. Until tomorrow you'll do your work in the ordinary way. Understand?"

"All right," I said, and she took, I thought, a particularly mean advantage of me.

"I shan't go out tonight. You've ruined my evening. When you make Julian's coffee tonight, bring me a cup of it. I shall be in the studio, I expect."

I assumed that she was emphasising the fact that I had been no more than a servant to her. It was true, after all.

"Very good," I said grimly, and left.

As soon as I reached the corridor, I saw we had raised the house. Mrs. Munsen was waiting for me at the top of the staircase, and I caught the flicker of Rudkin's coat tail.

My unnatural calm persisted. Luckily Mary Munsen appeared to understand, and when she insisted on bringing my evening meal on a tray to my room, she did not try to make me talk. She was a wise old woman. I think she knew how things were.

I felt frozen inside; I could not think, I could not plan, I could not even regret. I packed alone, refusing the help of the openly tearful Lily, and I worked on mechanically until I noticed that my travelling clock said a quarter to nine. I came alive then and realized just what was really happening. I was going away. It had ended in disaster. This was the last time——

By the time I reached the pantry I was crying so helplessly I hardly could fit the key into the lock. My first setback occurred when I found the light would not go on, and I assumed the bulb had burned out. By

44

leaving the door wide, I found I could get just enough of the corridor lighting to see what I was doing. Anyway, it hardly mattered, as my tears were blinding me and the place was as familiar as my hand.

I was furious with myself for crying, but I could not stop, and I dreaded going to Rita with my face swollen—or to Julian, either, for that matter. I prepared the two trays—Julian's little yellow one and another like it, only pink, for Rita. I had filled both cups and was counting Julian's tablets into his when I heard steps in the corridor. Mrs. Munsen long since had ceased to superintend my coffee-making, but I thought she had come along this evening to sympathise until I saw it was Rudkin.

"Light gone, miss?" he enquired, his tone as commiserating and regretful as his sister's had been. "Let's see." He hopped onto a stool with a surprising agility and touched the bulb, which came on immediately. "Only twisted," he reported cheerfully. "I came along, miss, because I wondered if you'd like me to take Mrs. Fayre's coffee to her."

So they had heard it all, had they? I was not surprised. Rita had a penetrating voice when she raised it. His kindness finished me, and I turned away so that he could not see my face.

"I don't know if she'd like that," I murmured.

"You leave that to me, miss." He sounded so very valiant.

"It's the p-pink tray," I sobbed, and I heard the cup rattle as he took it up and swept off with it. I followed blindly with the other, and I do not remember getting from the pantry to the music room; but when I entered, the lights were down and Julian was sitting alone with Stinker by the firelight.

"Mary?"

"No. It's me, Julian."

"Gillie." He got up at once, came over to me, and took the tray from my hands. I could not see his face, only his tall, thin figure bending toward me. I did not attempt to explain what had happened, but he answered me as though I had spoken. "I heard," he said. "I'm so sorry, Gillie. I do apologise for her."

There was something in the way he said it that was almost frightening. I caught a glimpse of his hatred, and its intensity surprised me.

"Drink your coffee before it gets cold," I said and watched him take the cup.

The firelight was flickering, and the pup sighed heavily, his nose between his paws.

I never can think of that moment without a thrill of pure terror.

It passed, the cup was back on its tray, and we stood near each other in the warm gloom. There was so much we needed to say and so very little we must.

"I shall go early in the morning," I said. "Good-bye."

"Good-bye, Gillie," he whispered steadily. He went with me to the door and held it open for me. As I passed him, he gave me an envelope.

"No refusals," he said quickly. "No, Gillie. Please. I couldn't bear it. You've got to take this just so I know you're all right until—until later on. Please, my dearest."

So I had the envelope crushed in my hand when I got to my room. It contained a check for two hundred and fifty pounds and a note to a bank manager instructing him to open an account for me.

I went to bed and tried to sleep. I never should see him, or the house, or Mrs. Munsen again, I thought. This was the end. But I was wrong.

At seven o'clock next morning the whole place was aroused by Mitzi's screaming. She had found Rita's bed empty, and on going down to the studio had discovered her lying there on the couch. She was cold by then; her eyes, their pupils contracted to pin points, were wide open. At her side was the cup on the pink tray, which I had sent her. It was empty.

Everybody knew. Everybody in the whole house knew at once, without being told, that Death was in that cup. Everybody, that is, except me. And I had prepared it.

I could not believe that Rita was dead, although Mitzi had shouted the information until it echoed up the stairs and down the corridors, dragging us all from our beds.

I tried to make sense of the screaming, and then, as the words slowly took shape, I scrambled up, threw on a dressing gown, and ran out to the head of the staircase.

It was still dark, of course, but the hall lights were on, and the cold dawn, appearing greyly at the tall windows, made the scene look different, oddly foreign and unnatural.

As I glanced down, I saw Rudkin come out of the studio. He was trembling, and there were bright spots of colour on his cheekbones. He was half supporting Mitzi, who looked about to faint.

She was a square, stolid woman, who ran to dark hair round the mouth despite a fantastic blonde creation on her head. But now she seemed to have grown old, and she walked uncertainly, as if she were not sure where she was going.

They were out in the centre of the floor before they suddenly looked up at me. I met two pairs of frightened eyes, but even then I did not recognize the suspicion there. I was shocked, but only by death. No hint of any further horror reached me, and it did not enter my head that I might be in any way involved.

"Is it true?" I asked.

Mitzi made an inarticulate sound and her eyes flashed at me. She opened her mouth to speak, but the old man silenced her.

"Go back to your room at once, miss," he said sharply to me. "Don't come down. It's no sight for you."

There was a startled peremptoriness in the order that was authoritative, but I only imagined he thought I should not interfere as I was not one of the family.

"But are you sure?" I persisted, glancing fearfully

47

toward the studio. "It doesn't seem possible. Are you sure, Rudkin, that she really is——"

Mitzi began to laugh horribly, and the old man shook her arm, silencing her abruptly.

"I am quite certain, miss," he said grimly. "Go back, if you please."

The whole house was alive by this time. Doors were opening, and I could hear hushed voices and sharp questions on all sides. I went slowly to my room and stood in the doorway, trying to guess what was happening from the rustlings and whisperings downstairs.

I assumed I was forgotten. It never occurred to me that the name on the lips of everyone who came out of that tomb of a studio was mine.

The realisation, when it did come, was terrifying. I was still in my dressing gown, lingering half in and half out of my bedroom, when there were soft footsteps on the stairs, and the next moment Julian came striding down the corridor toward me.

My first thought was that he looked like a skeleton again, his silk gown flapping round his long legs, his fair hair tousled, and his eyes pits of misery. There was something else in his eyes, too, part of which, thank God, was disbelief.

"Julian," I began eagerly, then was silent before his expression.

He caught my shoulders and thrust me into the room, closing the door behind him. "Gillie," he said huskily. "Oh, Gillie, what have you done?"

I drew back from his eyes, which were frightening in their wretchedness. "Done?" I echoed stupidly.

He put both hands on my shoulders, and his fingers bit into my flesh. I could feel his shaking, but his eyes never left mine. They peered searchingly into mine, determined yet dreading to see the truth there. "Gillie, my darling girl, what did you put in that cup?"

It took me a second or two to understand what he meant, and then I understood it all. I saw the whole thing clearly in one dreadful cinematic flash.

Rita had been poisoned. I had sent her a cup of coffee last thing at night. It is notorious that coffee disguises the taste of anything. The motive? Who than I had a better one?

For an instant, as the full realisation flooded over me, I was panic-stricken. I felt my eyes widening as Julian stared into them, and my mouth grew dry. Then, quite suddenly, it seemed absurd.

"Nothing," I said calmly. "Only coffee. That didn't kill her, Julian. You had some yourself."

My voice was very quiet; its naturalness comforted even me. I knew I was not guilty, nor even had I let the ghastly thought of doing it once creep through my mind.

He read something of my reasoning in my face, for I felt the tension go out of him, and he blinked at me like a man waking from a nightmare. "Oh, God bless you, Gillie," he said shakily. "Bless your glorious sanity, my dear. I'm desperately sorry. Forgive me. I ought to have known. The idea's too monstrous; I ought not to have credited it even for a moment. The whole thing has happened so suddenly that it's knocked all the sense out of me. At first there seemed to be no other explanation." His hands slid off my shoulders and took my hands.

"It's all right," I said, struggling to comfort him. "It's all right Julian. Only, don't go and get ill again. You see——"

My voice faded as the door behind us opened, and Mrs. Munsen stood there watching us. Julian let go my hands very slowly, and we both turned to face her.

It was obvious that she had been disturbed while dressing. The throat of her familiar frock was open, exposing an old-fashioned underbodice. The sight was somehow very shocking, and it emphasised the disaster in a way nothing else could have. Her face was chalky save for a network of tiny veins, and her mouth twisted, when she spoke. Her words were unexpected, and they shook me. She was not even angry, she was frightened.

"The doctor's on his way, Master Julian," she muttered. "For the love of God, boy, go out of this room. Don't be seen with her now."

Had she taken us by the shoulders and knocked our heads together, she could not have brought our position home to us more clearly.

Julian winced, and then the colour poured up over his face. "All right, Mary," he said. "I'll go now." But before he went, he took my hands again and looked down at me earnestly. "Don't be frightened, Gillie, and for heaven's sake, forgive me. It will be all right, darling, I swear it will. Try not to worry."

Mrs. Munsen stood holding the door for him. I could see that she was listening for any new sound downstairs; her very poise betrayed the urgency she felt. She sighed audibly, but unconsciously, as he left, but she did not follow him. Instead, she closed the door and put her back against it. For a moment she stood looking at me, her small black eyes oddly speculative. "Keep quiet, and I'll help you," she said distinctly.

I stared at her in amazement.

She ignored me and went on, still speaking in the same quiet, clear tone. "I'll help you all I can, and I'm not a fool, but don't you dare drag *him* into it. He never knew anything of this. I've known him ever since he was a baby, and no one will ever convince me different. Save him and I'll help you."

"But I know nothing of it either," I protested. "Honestly, Mrs. Munsen, you're wrong. You must believe me. I've done nothing."

She shook her head at me. "Keep quiet," she persisted. "Say nothing at all. That's your safest way."

"But you're being absurd."

"No." She opened the door and stood listening a moment. When she closed it again, she laid a finger on her lips. "They're all downstairs. You get dressed and stay here."

"Very well," I said, "but you're making a ridiculous mistake. There was nothing in that cup of coffee when it left my hands. For God's sake, Mrs. Munsen, do I look like a murderess?"

Her reply silenced me and sent a thin, cold trickle through my heart. "You had so much to gain," she said flatly. "I hated her, too, but I'm not young and I'm not in love. Keep your head, keep quiet, and keep him out of it. I'll help you."

With that she left me, and I crept slowly into my clothes, feeling cold and sick with apprehension. That calm assumption of my guilt was something I never had envisaged.

I think I expected the police to come and arrest me there and then, but my first visitor was old Dr. Crupiner.

He came tottering along the corridor, and I got a chair for him before I even spoke, he looked so old and unsteady. He sank into it gratefully and looked up at me with faded, trouble-filled eyes. "A tragedy," he said. "A great tragedy, Miss Brayton. They've told you, of course?"

"Yes," I said. "I can hardly believe it. She was so—so well yesterday when I saw her."

He nodded. "Poor lady. She was so wonderfully strong. Remarkably full of vitality. I don't think I've ever met anyone with greater energy, and now——God bless my soul! It doesn't bear thinking of." His conceit had vanished under the shock, and he was more human than I ever had known him to be.

"What was it?" I demanded. "Why did it happen?"

He came back to earth with a start and sat eyeing me dubiously. "Miss Brayton, I must talk to you very seriously. You made her some coffee last night, I understand?"

"Yes. Or, at least, she had some of the coffee I made for Colonel Fayre."

"Out of the same pot?"

"Yes."

"Did he drink his?"

"Yes, I saw him."

"Ah." He was silent for a time. "Miss Brayton," he began at last, "we have sent for the police, and I do not know if I am exceeding my authority by telling you this, but—ah—I have made up my mind to confide in you. In my opinion, there is absolutely no doubt that Mrs. Fayre met her death from an overdose of some very powerful narcotic after drinking the coffee last night, and there is absolutely no evidence that she administered it herself."

"No evidence?" I murmured stupidly.

"No phial," he said. "No box. No one has any knowledge of her possessing any drugs. I myself have attended her recently, and I should say she was the last person ever to have recourse to anything of that kind."

"Then you think that whatever it was was in the coffee?"

"My dear young lady, I don't know. I don't think anything. I remember only that Mrs. Fayre once told me that you were thought to be a little vague at times, a little absent-minded."

"No," I protested. "No. Besides, how could I? Where could I get such a thing? Oh no, Dr. Crupiner, there was nothing in the coffee I sent her."

He got up stiffly and sighed. I only half understood that he was trying to show me a way out. "That means you're accusing Rudkin, you know," he said gently.

"But of course I'm not!" I ejaculated. "I'm not accusing anyone. I don't believe it's happened. I don't see how it could."

He shook his head at me just as Mary Munsen had done. "Think," he said softly. "Just think it all out very carefully. Yes, Rudkin?"

The butler had tapped at the door and now put his head in. He did not look at me. The doctor appeared to expect him.

"I will come down," he said. "They're here, are they? Miss Brayton, you will oblige me by staying exactly where you are for the time being. Good-bye. I shall see you again."

He went out with a great deal of dignity, and I was left alone once more. I did my best to hang onto sanity.

I realised it must be a mistake, just as Julian had said, but it was a very frightening one. I hoped the police would hurry and make the real explanation clear to everyone. That was with the logical part of my mind; the rest, the emotional part, was just frightened, and my premonition of danger was very strong.

It seemed hours before the police came to see me. The winter sunshine was strong that morning, and it lighted up the room with a wistful, watery brightness and fell on my packed suitcases, making them look shabbier than ever. At last there was a knock. I opened the door at once and stepped back to admit the man who stood there.

He was not in the least what I had expected. There was nothing of the stolid, keen-eyed British policeman about him. He was thin and a little bent, with a neat grey head and shabby, tidy clothes. He wandered in without speaking, and I saw a face frankly ugly but not unengaging, with a wide mouth, too full of teeth, and pale, kindly eyes.

"You'll be Gillian Brayton," he said in a deep, quiet voice, which was not in the least alarming, and then added devastatingly, "The girl who made the coffee."

I glanced at him sharply. He was smiling a little, but I did not respond. "Yes, I made it."

"And you're sort of companion-help here, but no one knows what your duties are, except that you make coffee," he continued, looking around the room, his eyes taking in every detail.

I did not know what to reply to that, so I kept silent. It was true in a way, of course, but it sounded extraordinary when he put it so baldly.

"And you've got the sack."

"No," I protested hastily. "Not exactly. I—I resigned last night."

"Resigned," he echoed flatly, and I began to fear him. He possessed singleness of purpose; he was going somewhere, looking for something and all the ordinary side issues of human relationships did not interest him. He sat down suddenly on my bed and looked up at me, his head lolling back, his great toothy mouth jutting forward. "Tell me how you made the coffee," he said. His tone was affable and slightly condescending.

I told him all about it going over each point in detail.

He listened attentively. "She died after drinking it, you know," he said.

"So they told me."

"Who did?" That came very sharply.

"The doctor and Mrs. Munsen." I remembered just in time that it might be better not to mention Julian's name.

"That's the housekeeper? Nice old girl. Wasn't brokenhearted to hear her mistress was dead. Nor are you, are you?"

The final question came so directly that it made me jump. "I haven't quite realised it's happened yet," I said truthfully.

"No, I don't suppose you have. Who do you imagine I am?"

"A police inspector."

"Wrong. Superintendent. Higher grade. The housekeeper tell you I was coming?"

"No. The doctor told me that."

He sighed, and unfolded himself lazily. "I get a lot of help," he said so drily that I almost smiled, and then saw that he was expecting it of me. "Never mind, you're right, in the main. The name is Alexander McNaught, Divisional Superintendent. A very remarkable man in many ways."

I did smile at that, and he seemed surprised.

"There is little amusing about me," he said seriously. "It's my job to ask questions. We'll go and inspect this pantry of yours. Is it correct that you have the only key?"

"I believe so." I showed him the key lying where I always kept it in a small porcelain bowl on my mantel.

He took it without enthusiasm and compared it with

54

the one belonging to the room. It was not the same, and he shrugged.

"Not every lock in the house is identical, anyway. That's one small dispensation. Come along. You lead the way."

There were two or three people in the hall—a plain-clothes detective or so and a uniformed constable, who all gave me the same ostentatiously disinterested stare; and Rudkin, who smiled at me stoutly. So he was on my side. That was something.

The door of the studio was shut. I glanced at its shining panels and guessed what must lie behind them. It was the first time I really comprehended that Rita was dead, I think, and I suppose I swayed a little, for McNaught put a hand on my shoulder.

"No need to get seasick yet," he said. "The boat hasn't started. Is this the door?" He unlocked it and stood aside for me to enter. "Keep your arms to your sides. Don't touch anything. Now, just tell me again exactly what you did the last time you were in here."

I repeated the story as carefully as I could, indicating each utensil as I mentioned it. The little room was sunny now; the bright colours of paint and china glistened familiarly with innocent prettiness. When I came to the point at which I counted out the tablets, he stopped me.

"Where's the bottle?"

"There." I pointed to the phial. It was in its accustomed place, right in front of the first shelf, just as I had left it. As my glance fell on it, my heart jumped. The bottle looked exactly the same. It was just about as full as it ought to have been, and I saw the small white tablets showing faintly through the coloured glass. But the label was wrong. The inscription was written in a spiky hand, but not quite the same one, and there was less of it. As I bent forward to read it, McNaught did too.

"*Mrs. Fayre. The Tablets. One when pain is most severe.*"

"Oh, my God!" I heard the exclamation as if someone else had muttered it, and McNaught caught me round the shoulders.

"What's the matter?"

"It's wrong," I muttered, pointing to the bottle. "It's different. It's not Julian's."

He turned me round to face him, his eyes hard and inquisitive. "Are these the tablets you used last night?"

"I—don't know." Having made the admission, I had to explain. "It was dark. I told you. I've been giving these tablets to Colonel Fayre every night for weeks. It's the only bottle of tablets here, and only I use the pantry. I—I don't read the label every time—why should I? I don't see what has happened. Where did this come from?"

"You are not prepared to swear that this was not the bottle you used last night?"

"No. No, but——"

"But what?"

"But it was Julian's cup in which I put the tablets. I took it to him myself. These seem to be Rita's, don't they? It says 'Mrs. Fayre.'"

"It would seem so," he drawled, and bent forward again to peer at a squiggle at the foot of the label. It was a date, I thought. I could not read it.

McNaught made something of it, for, still keeping hold of me, he shouted down the corridor for Rudkin. The old man came at once, as if he had been waiting for the summons. He looked like a withered ghost blown along by a fitful wind.

McNaught showed him the bottle. "Don't touch that," he commanded, "but look at it. Ever seen it before?"

I was certain Rudkin was going to deny it, and his reaction amazed me. He read the line aloud in an uncertain old voice, and then stood up, blank astonishment on his face.

"God Almighty, sir," he said.

"Recognize it?"

56

"Yes, sir. I thought it had been destroyed. When I last saw it, it was in my wife's hand."

"Your wife's? But she's dead, isn't she? Didn't you tell me you were a widower?"

"I did, sir, and I have been one for three years. My wife used to live here. She was old Mrs. Fayre's personal maid."

McNaught expelled a long breath. "Old Mrs. Fayre died before her, then? She was the Mrs. Fayre referred to on this label?"

"Yes, sir. That was the old mistress's medicine."

"I see." He paused and looked from one to the other of us. "Did you know about that?" he enquired of me.

"No," I told him.

He sighed and returned to Rudkin. "Well, now. We're talking about three years ago. When your wife showed you this, did she say anything about it? Try to remember exactly."

Rudkin was unexpectedly clear. His eyes, which were black like his sister's, were excited yet remarkably guiltless. It was plain that he was genuinely curious, and anxious to help. "It was the day after the poor missus' funeral," he said. "We were all very low, and poor Harriet was crying as she tidied up. I came in on her when she was sorting out the poor lady's things. She showed me this bottle and said what wonderful stuff it was, and how she'd be grateful to the doctor as long as she lived for giving it to the mistress. She said it wiped the pain away."

"Was that the doctor I saw this morning?"

"No, sir. His brother. He was gone, too, the poor old gentleman, before the year was out."

"Dead too?" McNaught was exasperated.

"Yes, sir. Him and the missus and Harriet all in one year."

"Very sad, I'm sure. What did your wife propose to do with the bottle? Do you know?"

"I don't, sir. I told her to give it back to the doctor, in case it was dangerous."

"She doesn't seem to have done so."

"Apparently not, sir."

"What do you think she did with it?"

Rudkin glanced up, and his black eyes were quick and speculative. "Knowing Harriet, I think she hid it, sir, somewhere in the house, thinking it might come in useful sometime. She was like that, was Harriet."

"Have you ever seen it since?"

"No, sir. Never. Not till now."

McNaught was not satisfied. "I find that curious," he said. "A thing doesn't lie about a house for three years without someone's noticing it."

"It might if it was hidden, sir. It's a big house."

The superintendent hunched his shoulders. He was growing more and more depressed. "Maybe," he agreed. "One more question. You don't happen to know what this *is*, do you?"

"I think I do, sir." The old man's face was working in his excitement. "I believe it's morphia. That's what Harriet said it was."

McNaught turned away from him and looked thoughtfully at me. "And you, Miss Brayton," he murmured, "do you happen to know offhand what is the fatal dose of morphia?"

"No," I breathed.

He went on looking at me curiously, almost quizzically. "I wonder," he said.

I spent the rest of that day in my room. They kept me there. I was not under arrest, merely invited to stay there, and a plain-clothes man was stationed in the corridor to see that I accepted the invitation.

No one from the rest of the household was permitted to see me. When Lily, who was all of a flutter, I suspect, came hurrying up with some breakfast for me, the detective insisted on helping her, with all the appearance of being obliging. He was a large, sloppy person with gentle eyes and a smile, and he sent her down and brought the tray to me. But when I told him

I would pour him some coffee if he got himself a cup, he gave me a rather curious look.

However, McNaught had reckoned without Mrs. Munsen. There was a hot linen press in my bathroom, whose floor boards took out, so that one could see down into the kitchen cupboard where the tea towels were drying. I heard her tapping in there soon after Lily had gone down, and I went in to find her standing on a chair to look up at me.

"I'm here," she said, as if that were everything. "Don't you go and get frightened. He doesn't know where he is yet."

"What's happening?" I whispered.

"She's been taken away," she murmured back. "He's in the studio making an office of it and having us in one after the other asking questions. Cook's gone now."

"Has the doctor gone home?"

"Yes. Rudkin heard them talking in the hall. Something about looking up his brother's records. We're all saying we didn't know about the bottle Harriet kept."

"Is that true?"

"Yes, of course it is. We shan't go lying. That Mitzi's making trouble. They caught her phoning to Dr. Phoebus."

"Has he come round?"

"Not yet. Miss Gillie——"

"Yes?"

"You'll remember what I told you. Keep Mister Julian out of it, dear. He's not strong enough to stand it. Promise me."

"Yes." I made the word resolute. "I promise you."

She withdrew then, and I went back to the window, where I stood pressing my forehead against the cold pane and striving to think clearly. Whatever I had done, it had been a mistake. Surely, I thought, they must see that. People weren't convicted unjustly, not nowadays. Circumstantial evidence wasn't everything; besides, there was so little of that, unless they got hold of a motive.

There was no point in deceiving myself about the

motive. I had the best one in the world, or I would have if Julian and I had not been the people we were. As it was, there was nothing between us, nothing that conceivably could be falsely construed.

Nothing. And then, and only then, did I remember the check and the letter to the bank manager. I had not thought of them since the night before.

I went shakily across the room to the lowboy where my bag lay. I could not believe I had been such a fool as to forget them; but I had, and what was worse, I had left them in the room when I went down to the pantry with the superintendent. My fingers were so unsteady I could hardly get the bag open, and when at last I did and stared into its empty depths, I was cold to my bones.

They had searched the room and found them, and now the damning things were downstairs for anyone to draw conclusions from.

When lunchtime came, the detective brought me another tray. "We have to save the lady's steps," he said with a heavy jocularity that would not have deceived a baby.

I could not eat, and I could not think. If I had been guilty, I might at least have been able to plan. As it was, I was helpless. I thought about Julian and found myself praying that, whatever happened, the experience would not make him ill again. I don't think I remembered Rita at all.

It was nearly three when at last they came for me. The room was in shadow, and I was stiff and chilly when the detective put his head in to tell me I was wanted.

"Now it's coming. Now they're going to arrest me." The words sounded as clearly in my ears as if I had spoken them. I wondered if I ought to appeal to anybody, or if Uncle Grey's old solicitors would appear for me. Remembering them, I thought I might almost be better off if they refused.

The first thing I saw as I entered the studio was the

envelope that had contained Julian's check. It lay on the
mirror-topped table, which the superintendent had made
his desk. It was set there so prominently I knew he
intended me to see it.

I picked it up. "This was in my bag."

He raised his eyebrows. "We're keeping it safe," he
said drily. He was sitting behind the table on one of the
white Empire chairs, which made him look dustier than
ever, and presently he grinned at me. It was not the
reception I had expected, and his opening gambit was
surprising too. "Ever tried to find anything in this
house?"

"No, I don't think so."

"Never lost anything in it, I suppose. Well, I shan't
buy that one. We have lost two things, Miss Brayton,
and although we've searched the bric-a-brac, we can't
find either of them yet."

His glance wandered round the room, and I saw it
once more in all its grey-and-white modernity. The
bottles in the old bookcases were rather vulgar, just as
Ferdie had said. I noticed it again absurdly, at such a
time.

McNaught returned to me. "The first thing we want
is a second key to the pantry, if there ever was one. It's
a more unusual lock than I thought. No other key in the
house turns it."

"I've never seen one like it," I said slowly. "But mine
used to lie in the bowl all day."

"You were packing in your room yesterday evening
from half-past six until a quarter to nine?"

"Yes, about that."

"No one borrowed it between those hours, then. The
other thing I'd like to find is the luminal."

"Luminal?"

"The original bottle of tablets. Colonel Fayre's sedative."

"Oh, was it that? I'm afraid I didn't know," I said
truthfully, but added, as the utter absurdity of the thing
overcame me: "But it was there in the pantry last night.

It must have been. I gave Julian four tablets; I put them in his coffee, and I saw him drink it."

"You told me that before." He was resigned rather than contemptuous, and his pleasant, ugly face looked regretful. "Sit there," he said, pointing to a chair near the table. "I want to talk to you about something else. By the way, you realize we're making notes, don't you?"

I did. I had seen the man with the fountain pen the moment I went in. "Yes," I said, "I saw that."

"You're a very cool young woman."

"I don't feel it."

He cocked an inquisitive eye at that and seemed more friendly. "I understand from Colonel Fayre that it was he who advised you to leave. Is that true?"

"Yes." Now it was coming.

"The reason he gives"—McNaught glanced at a pad in front of him and drawled the words pointedly—"the reason he gives is that he had formed an opinion you were growing too fond of him."

If he hoped that would rattle me, he was disappointed. I could not tell if that was all Julian had said or if he had said it at all. I was still cautious. "Is that what he thought?" I ventured.

"Don't you know?"

"He did not tell me so."

"Well, let's put it another way. Was it true?"

It was difficult. I did not know how much might depend on the answer.

"Was it true?"

"I like him very much," I said helplessly. "I like him well enough to go the moment he suggested it."

"Because you thought it prudent?"

"Because I—I wanted to help," I said.

"I see." McNaught leaned back in the slender chair, which protested dangerously. His announcement came out of the blue. "I understand that Colonel Fayre was under the impression that his wife had introduced you deliberately into the household in the hope that he would compromise himself with you."

"What!" I was out of my chair at that, all caution forgotten in my fury and surprise.

He waved me down again. "That's news to you, is it?"

"It's absurd. I was engaged because Rita could trust me. The doctor told me that in the beginning."

"He told me that too." McNaught was scratching his ear. "Other people prefer the second story."

"But what for?" I persisted. "Why should she want such a thing? What woman would?"

He watched me with pale eyes. "I wonder if anyone on earth is as innocent as you look," he said. "You're only twenty, of course, and 'nicely brought up,' as they say. It may not have occurred to you that a judge might see his way to excuse certain irregularities in a wife's behaviour and even so far forget himself as to award her thumping alimony if her husband betrayed her under her own roof."

"I don't believe it," I said. "I don't believe it of anyone, and I don't believe it of Rita. It's a filthy idea. Rita chose me because we were friends at school."

The pale eyes were calmly inquisitive. "A lot of difference in your ages," he remarked. "You could not have been great friends. You are only twenty now, and she has lived out of England several years, hasn't she?" He was so horribly right. I could feel the ground opening under my feet. His appalling suggestion explained so many things, especially my first reception in the house.

"That was the idea in Fayre's mind when he told you to go."

"No."

"How do you know?"

I saw the pitfall just in time. "He would have sent me away before, not now."

McNaught brought his chair down on all four legs. "Why did you twist the lamp bulb so that it would not light last night?"

"I didn't."

63

"Yet it was twisted, wasn't it? Rudkin put it right for you?"

"Yes."

"Light bulbs don't turn by themselves."

"I didn't do it. Why should I?"

He did not answer, but switched the subject with disconcerting suddenness. "Colonel Fayre did not dismiss you in the beginning because he was not afraid of you. You had begun to make headway at last."

"No."

"You say you were not in on it. You and Mrs. Fayre weren't in it together?"

"No."

"You mean you were in it with her?"

I was getting hopelessly confused, and I knew it. He had become an enemy and was slowly but surely wearing me down.

"Make up your mind. Which was it? You and she arranged the whole thing, and the Colonel saw through it last night. Is that right?"

"No."

"Then——"

"I beg your pardon, I had no idea anyone was in here." The soft voice from the doorway surprised everybody, I think.

McNaught paused in full flight and glared across the room, his eyes bright with irritation. "Who let you in?"

The abrupt question recalled the visitor, who was withdrawing, and Henri Phoebus reappeared. I was amazed by the change in him. He looked as if he had been through some long and terrible experience. His plump face was drawn, and his eyes looked heavy in their sockets. "I have been in the house some little time," he said, with a trace of his normal airiness.

"Isn't there anyone on this door?" demanded McNaught.

"At the moment, no. But I am sorry to intrude. I will withdraw at once. As I told you, I thought the room was unoccupied."

McNaught let him go but he followed him into the hall, and we heard him speaking sharply to the constable, who must have left his post for a moment. He returned immediately, but he did not resume his questioning. There was a new expression in his eyes. He looked puzzled and as if he were trying to recall something that had escaped him. "Who is that, do you know?" I told him, and he shook his head. "Phoebus?"

"I think he's quite well known—at least, Rita implied that to me. He was her entrepreneur."

"What the devil's that?"

"It's like an impresario, isn't it? She painted, you know."

"So I heard," he murmured absently. "That chap here a lot?"

"Quite often."

"Did he know her when she lived abroad?"

"I—" The words died on my lips as I caught his expression.

The idea that had come to him evidently had shaken him. He stood staring ahead of him, mingled incredulity and astonishment in his eyes.

"I don't know," I finished.

He looked at me vacantly for a minute. "No," he said at last. "No, you wouldn't. No, you go back to your bedroom and stay there. Here, Mason."

The man with the notebook rose and went to him, and I was forgotten for the time being; but as soon as I stepped out of the room, the fat detective was beside me again, and when we got upstairs, he resumed his vigil in the corridor. As I entered the bedroom, I caught sight of myself in the mirror. I looked as though I had been faded by a very bright light, and there were bones in my face I did not know I had.

I sat down and tried to sort it all out, but my reasoning was thrown into confusion by the one dreadful question that haunted me all the time and forced itself into my thoughts when they should have been clear and constructive.

Had Julian really thought that Rita and I——

I did not believe it, I could not believe it, but I did not know for sure. Julian never had told me in so many words that he loved me. Suppose that all the time I'd been horribly mistaken and that he was only being kind, while he thought——

I would not go on, I would not face it, but I had a little foretaste of hell up there in the dusk that winter's night.

It was a little later when my jailer tapped again. I thought he'd come to call me down for more questioning, but it was only to bring me yet another tray. He set it on the table and went out again, leaving me gaping at it. Not at the teapot nor the eggshell-china cup, but at the tray itself.

It was pink. Surely it was pink. It must be the one I had sent to Rita the night before. Yet I couldn't believe anyone would be so cruel as to rescue it from the studio after the poisoned cup had been removed from it and to have sent it to me.

I took the tea things off it and switched on the light. Now I could see that the tray was yellow. And the truth—or at least a part of it—glimmered faintly in my mind.


I decided to wait until after midnight; before then I dared not risk it. I intended to go down to the studio and look at the tray, if it hadn't been taken away.

It was a grim vigil up there in the bright little room which I had come to love so much. The tray lay where I had left it, and every now and then I glanced at it, and each time I felt more certain I was right.

About ten o'clock I heard a tapping from the linen cupboard, and I hurried in to find Mrs. Munsen standing on the chair looking up at me.

"That superintendent's gone at last," she whispered. "He went off ten minutes ago, saying you were not to be disturbed."

"Did he take the others?"

"No, they're still here, but they won't stay all night, surely? Rudkin thinks they'll likely leave one man in the hall to watch us, but you can't tell with them. I'm going to bed. I'm dead on my feet."

"You must be," I said absently.

I was wondering how I could ask her about something. A favour, but the request stuck in my throat.

"Dr. Phoebus has taken himself off too," she whispered. "I told him straight this wasn't the right house for visitors. He went off like a whipped dog. He's been all over the place today, like he was demented. Lily found him in *her* bedroom once."

"In Rita's room?" I said with surprise.

"Yes. He'd got part of the carpet rolled back, if you please, and all he did when Lily stared at him was to ask her if the police were still in the studio."

"He hasn't been in there, then?" I asked quickly, my thoughts flying to the tray.

"He has not," she agreed grimly and began to climb down. "He and Mitzi have been whispering in corners all day. There's something between those two we don't know of, if you ask me. They're looking for something. Well, good night, miss, and don't forget what I told you."

"Oh, please wait," I murmured hurriedly, thankful she could not see the colour in my face. "Mrs. Munsen, could you—could I ask you to take a note to the Colonel?"

She was suspicious immediately. I could feel her eyeing me fiercely in the cupboard's gloom. "What do you want to say to him?"

I didn't know. The awful thing was, I didn't know. I only wanted to get some response, some little reassurance. It was madness, of course. I knew it and I was ashamed of it. But more than my own safety, more than anything else in the world, I wanted to know that the things McNaught had implied were not true.

She was waiting for an answer, and the last thing I intended to do was antagonise her. A possible excuse occurred to me. "I—I wanted to tell him that they know about that check," I explained.

To my astonishment she laughed very softly. "He's heard all about that."

"How do you know? Did he—did he tell you?"

"No. I heard them questioning him."

"Mrs. Munsen, how could you have heard? Where were they?"

"In the studio," she said calmly. "There's way and means of hearing things in this house if you know them."

Her admission of eavesdropping was perfectly complacent. I understood then that Julian was still a child to her; she had no scruples whatever where his welfare was concerned.

"What did he tell them?" I demanded breathlessly.

"The truth, of course," she said contemptuously. "There's no need for *him* to lie. He told them he wouldn't turn any girl out into the world without a penny."

It sounded terribly cold.

"It was a lot of money," I murmured.

"That's what they said," she agreed, "and they tried to make it sound very unpleasant. But he soon put them in their places. He said he was a rich man and wasn't in the habit of doing things by halves."

"Is that all he told them?"

"It's all I'm repeating, miss, and I'm not taking any notes to him. The master's gone to his bed, and by now he's asleep in it, please God. If I were you, I should do the same."

I heard her step down off the chair, and I knelt on the floor and strained my eyes after her. "Mrs. Munsen," I said. "I didn't do it."

There was silence for a moment, and then her voice came to me, grim through the darkness. "I'm not sorry it's done," she said. "You go to bed and keep your head. Say your prayers, if you're not afraid to."

\*     \*     \*

At eleven o'clock the fat detective went away. At least, when I looked out my door, there was for the first time no sign of his solid bulk in the corridor. So I knew there was only the other man to be considered, the one Rudkin thought they would leave on duty in the hall.

All the same, I was very jumpy. Several times I thought I heard footsteps in the corridor, but always when I sprang to look there was no one there.

I turned the lights off in the passage, finally, but still I was not certain I was quite alone in the wing. Once I thought I saw a flicker of something that might have been a skirt or a coat disappearing round the end of the corridor.

I undressed and lay down on my bed to wait. I thought if I waited till late enough, I could slip past the man in the hall and get into the studio.

At a quarter to twelve I turned out the light and sat in the dark. I dared not think of Julian. With the darkness all my fears had become intensified, and I felt deserted as well as trapped. Nobody came near me, and there was no sound.

When the clock of the church on the other side of the river struck one and the lazy musical chime of the hour had died away across the water, I summoned all my courage, opened my door, and stepped out.

The house smelled warm and sweet with polish and the scents of wood and potpourri. I was still in the old dressing gown I had had at school, and I had taken off my shoes so that I could feel my way silently over the rugs and the parquet in the hall.

The whole world seemed to be in darkness. There was no gleam of light anywhere. The curtains were drawn and the street lamps shut out. The only sounds I heard, as I stood listening, were the aggressive tick of the grandfather clock at the head of the staircase and the thudding of my own heart.

I was so busy concentrating on finding out if there was anyone watching in the hall, and if so, where exactly he sat, that I was not listening for any sound behind me.

I reached the stairhead without making a rustle. The folds of my woollen gown were noiseless, and my bare feet sank quietly into the thick carpet.

It was when I was halfway down that a stair cracked loudly behind me and I thought I heard someone breathing. Only my grip on the banister prevented me from falling. I looked back over my shoulder, and the darkness wreathed and contracted as I stared into it. I was sure there was a deeper black in the shadow than there should have been, and for a moment I stood frozen, almost too frightened to breathe.

I moved on at last, but I was terrified now, and aware of each separate and particular hair stiffening in the dark as my scalp crawled.

At last my foot touched the cold parquet of the hall. Once again I stood quiet, straining my ears. I was terrified, both of what might be behind me and of the watcher I imagined might be ahead.

But this time there was no sound, nothing; only the ticking of the angry old clock behind me in the dark. I still had a long way to go. The hall was wide and the studio door was at the far end of it. I let go the baluster and stepped into the blackness.

It was at that moment that I heard the sigh. It was very distinct, very human, and horribly close, just behind and a little above me.

I swung round, my heart in my mouth. As I turned, my bare foot squeaked on the polished wood, and an instant later a flashlight beam, wide and white and inescapable, shot up from the studio doorway. It held us both, me and the man at my heels.

I saw the man behind me was Julian at the moment his arms went round me. I saw his scared, imploring eyes and his mouth set in a hard line. Then I was aware of only the arms biting into me and the sudden blessed peace as my body pressed against the cool silk of his dressing gown.

I felt him tremble, and the flashlight beam grew shorter.

As I opened my lips, he put his hand over my mouth and I was quiet. He was hurting me unconsciously, and suddenly I knew that I liked it and that he, too, felt just as I did with the same reckless surge of pain.

So it was then, at that most hopeless of all moments, that I understood at last about me and Julian, so that all my doubt vanished and the ache at my heart disappeared.

I knew now who it was who had been near me all the evening when I thought I was alone in the ghostly wing of the house, and who it was I nearly had seen turning the corner of the corridor. I knew it was Julian who had kept watch on my door after the detective had gone, and he who had waited near at hand in case there was trouble and I needed him. It was good to know that.

Meanwhile, the beam came closer, holding us squarely in its broad shaft, and peering into the gloom behind it, I made out McNaught's face above the light.

To my surprise he made no attempt to speak, but signalled us to keep quiet. Over my head Julian nodded. McNaught grinned ferociously, and the light went out.

For what was perhaps three minutes, although it felt like hours, we waited. It was perfectly black, and I could make out nothing in the shadows. I had no idea what was happening or what was coming, and I lay back content against Julian, his arms still round me, his heart thudding against my shoulder, his breath fanning my hair.

Suddenly McNaught spoke; his deep voice sounded sharp in the darkness. "Now," he said.

The next moment the door of the studio clattered open, and there was a rush of feet. McNaught had a number of police with him. They had been concealed in the dark hall, waiting for something to happen inside the studio, and I, with Julian trailing me, had come down into the very midst of the ambush.

The crowd of policemen swept us on into the room where Rita had died.

The vast room was cold and gloomy. The only light came from the hearthrug, where a flashlight lay burning, casting its misshapen beam across the floor and up the wall.

I think it was a curtain I noticed first after that moment of complete bewilderment. It was streaming out in the strong draught. Under it there came climbing in through the low, wide-open window the fat detective who had been guarding me upstairs.

Then I saw Henri Phoebus. He was kneeling on the hearthrug, his arm thrust deeply into a small cupboard which had appeared in the panelling just under the right-hand built-in bookcase where the bottles and glasses were kept. I never had suspected its existence. It had been hidden in the moulding.

All the same, I don't think it was so much a secret cupboard as a forgotten one. Old Mrs. Fayre and Harriet had kept the Minton in the bookcase and never had permitted anyone to approach it, so it was unlikely that anyone else in the household knew of the hiding place below it.

When I caught sight of Henri Phoebus, it was in the instant of his first surprise. His pallid face wore a grotesque expression of alarm, and in its arrested movement his plump body looked stiff and unreal, like a waxwork.

I was the first person he recognised. He knelt staring at me for a moment and then scrambled to his feet and came for me. "You," he screamed. "You killed her. You knew!"

As I drew back, I felt Julian's arm tighten round me, and he swung me out of the way. In the same second the fat detective lunged forward and tackled Phoebus round the knees. They went down together, and immediately a ring of police closed in on them.

Just then someone behind us turned up the light, and the room became familiar again in the glare. The room was so full of Rita's personality that I was violently aware of her. It seemed incredible that she should not be there, forceful and didactic as ever. I shivered.

Meanwhile, McNaught had stepped round the struggling group on the carpet to examine the cupboard, and presently he came to me holding something on his palm.

"Look," he said, his pleasant, ugly face glowing with satisfaction. "That's more like it, isn't it?"

I stared at it. It was Julian's bottle of luminal tablets.

"And here's the key," he continued, producing it. "They were in there together. That's got the whole thing taped, I think."

I looked at the key curiously. It was a new one, a fellow to the pantry key I possessed.

"That's the evidence," McNaught said cheerfully. "That's just exactly what we want."

By this time Phoebus had ceased to protest. He was crouching on the floor shivering. His captor jerked him to his feet. He made no further attempt to accuse me, but his eyes never left my face, and I turned away before the fury in their depths.

McNaught ignored him. He glanced across the room to where a square, middle-aged detective stood waiting impassively.

"You'll take over now, George," he said. "You know the charge?"

The inspector nodded briskly. "You can leave it to me, Mac. Attempted murder—accessory before—okay?"

"*Attempted* murder," I ejaculated. "But——"

McNaught took me firmly by the elbow and led me through the crowd, out of the room, and into the hall. Julian came with us, keeping close to my side, and out of the corner of my eye I saw the inspector bearing down on Phoebus.

"Attempted murder of the Colonel, of course," said McNaught when we were out of earshot. "That chap is an accessory before the fact, so they'll probably make it conspiracy. And now, Miss Brayton," he went on with

73

sudden fierceness, "what the blazes do you think you were doing creeping down on us and almost wrecking the whole night's work? It didn't occur to you, I suppose, that if we hadn't caught him with the evidence, we shouldn't have had a thing against him."

"I came to look for the tray," I said.

"The tray?" His voice sharpened, and his big grey eyes regarded me curiously. "When did you think that one out?"

I was still puzzled and a little afraid. I glanced at Julian. "I don't understand," I said. "Do you? Who killed Rita?"

McNaught paused before us, his untidy teeth appearing in a ferocious smile. "You did, Miss Brayton," he said steadily, and added after an appreciable pause, "I think."

I felt Julian stiffen at my side, and at the same moment I saw the full depths of the tragedy.

They were going to prove that I had made a mistake and that in my wretched carelessness I had used tablets from a phial whose label I had not read. I was going to escape; but in that case, there never could be any real happiness for Julian and me. Whatever happened now, whatever we decided to do, wherever we decided to travel, Rita always would be there, dark and hard and beautiful, standing between us like a grim shadow.

I met Julian's eyes, and in their darkness I read my own thoughts echoed.

McNaught's deep voice cut into the silence. "If you've a fire going anywhere, we'll have a spell before it if you don't mind," he said. "It's turned remarkably cold. I don't know if you've noticed it."

We sat in the music room. The fire was almost out; but Rudkin, who looked particularly unlike his formal self in a dusty brown dressing gown and muffler, brought bundles of kindling and made a blaze that filled the warm dusk of the room with the smell of resin.

Meanwhile, Mrs. Munsen, fully dressed, fluttered about like a lean black bat, handing hot toddy on a silver tray. The two old servants had appeared the moment Julian needed them, like genii of the house. I was vividly aware that their anxiety was as sharp as mine; their fortunes were bound with Julian's, their happiness was dependent on his.

McNaught was as bright and dominant as he had been all day. The man was tireless. He sat in the deep leather chair opposite us and sniffed his glass appreciatively. We remained looking at him warily.

It was some time before he spoke. I was not sure if he was deliberating or simply waiting for the old brother and sister to withdraw. They went at last, but I remembered what Mrs. Munsen had said about there being ways and means of hearing in this house, and I wondered if she was so very far away.

Finally the superintendent spoke, and his words turned our world over for us. "You've got to face it, Colonel Fayre, and it's not a pleasant fact. She was not your wife." He spread his feet out to the blaze and gave us time to take in the full meaning of the astounding statement.

I glanced nervously at Julian. He was sitting up stiffly in his wing chair, the skin drawn tightly over the fine bones of his face and his eyes narrow and incredulous. "Not my wife?"

McNaught's pleasant, ugly face was unexpectedly sympathetic. "No, sir. She was not your wife. I can understand this is going to be a considerable shock to you, but it's one of those things that can't be put too plainly. She was Mrs. Henri Phoebus."

I felt I was going to laugh. I don't know why, but it was as though some unbearable bond had snapped and set me free. My hand found Julian's, and he held it very tight.

"I did not know that," he said.

"No, sir. I don't suppose you did."

McNaught's voice was still unwontedly gentle. "But I hope you'll forgive me if I say I think you're well out of it. I want to put the whole thing to you straight. It's one of those simple stories that look complicated from the middle, but if you start at the beginning, it ravels out like a skein."

I was still in the dark. The way McNaught was speaking suggested that there was still some ray of hope for us; but the one overwhelming and dreadful fact still remained, and it obsessed me.

"But you said I killed her," I murmured huskily.

He turned to peer at me where I sat on a fireside stool between Julian and the hearth. His eyes were kindly, but there was no weakening there. "You did, miss," he insisted gravely, and added after the same pause, "I think."

I closed my eyes so as not to see him, but I heard Julian stir as he leaned forward toward the man. "Were they crooks, Superintendent?" he said softly.

McNaught met his gaze with a flicker of appreciation. "Yes, sir," he said quietly. "Two of the cleverer kind."

"But that's not possible," I burst out. "I knew Rita at school, and——"

McNaught shook his head at me. "It's been years since she was at school," he said. "It doesn't take that long to step off the white line. Maybe I'd better let you have the story as I know it. I've had several good men at work to get this information in the time, but I've checked it and it's accurate. I'm going to write my report when I leave here, so perhaps I'll give you a little résumé. It'll help me as well as you."

Julian motioned to him to continue. He was paler than I ever had seen any man, and his eyes were grim.

"Well," McNaught settled himself. "These are the facts as far as we've been able to trace them. Ten years ago, when Rita Raven left her boarding school, she went abroad to live with her mother, who had parted from her husband. The mother was a reckless type, a hopeless gambler, and when her daughter picked up with Henri Phoebus and married him, she does not seem to have raised much objection. Mother and daughter parted then." He paused, choosing his words as if he already were writing his report. "At that time," he went on presently, "Phoebus was a small con man in Paris. He was nothing to look at, but he was attractive to women, although Rita Raven seems to have been the only one to make any real impression on him. They struck up a partnership, and with her help he blossomed out into bigger things."

"You had seen him before," I put in, as the inspiration came to me. "You recognised him when he came into the studio this afternoon."

"Ah, you noticed that, did you?" He eyed me approvingly. "Yes, I recognised him, but not immediately. I don't forget faces, though—that's part of my success. When I first saw Phoebus, I was in Monaco, working with the Sûreté on the Le Grand case, and a French inspector pointed him out to me as we sat in a café. He said he was one of their more interesting criminals. As soon as I caught sight of him today, I knew his face was familiar, but I couldn't place him until you said he called himself Mrs. Fayre's entrepreneur."

"How do you mean? I don't understand that." Julian spoke sharply, and I realised what an intolerable experience this revelation must be to him.

"It was the word the man from the Sûreté used," McNaught explained. "He was describing the racket Phoebus and his wife were suspected of running. It was a curious business, I remember. She was quite a clever painter in her way, and she used to produce some rather questionable modern pictures, which in turn attracted a questionable type of crowd to the select little shows they gave. It was all very expensive and affected, and yet rather nasty. I needn't put it clearer than that, need I?"

Julian shook his head, and we listened in fascinated silence as the deep voice rumbled on.

"When the woman had attracted the likely birds, Henri Phoebus picked his victims. His method was quite simple. He presented himself as a special type of psychoanalyst and gradually collected a small and wealthy clientele. His manner was charming, and he ingratiated

77

himself easily with a certain type of rich, silly, and slightly vicious elderly woman. They abound in certain European capitals. They went to him to talk about themselves and it was all very private and confidential to begin with. Phoebus learned many secrets. After that——" He shrugged. "It was just straight blackmail. Vienna, Monte Carlo, and Madrid were all too hot to hold them at one time. They certainly got around."

Julian moved in his chair, and I was desperately sorry for him. Even McNaught cleared his throat, the first sign of embarrassment I had noticed in him.

"Early in the war they came to London," he began slowly, then added abruptly, "I don't want to hurt your feelings, sir, but it's now my duty to put a delicate matter to you as frankly as I can."

"You're being the soul of kindness to me, Superintendent," Julian murmured, and the edge on his tone was not hidden from me, although McNaught missed it. "Please go on."

"Well, sir, I have to remind you that when you first met this—er—lady, you were a young Commando officer just off overseas. You were a wealthy man and an attractive youngster, if I may say so, but, quite frankly, at that time your chances of coming back alive were not particularly bright. Isn't that so?"

"Yes. Oh, yes. That's true enough." Julian let the words fall absently. He was making up his mind to say something he found difficult. I knew him so well that I could feel him hesitate, struggling to master his reluctance. "McNaught," he said at last. "This isn't very easy to say, and I'm afraid I may not make myself clear. But I wonder if you'll understand if I tell you that I knew Rita was several years older than I was and that it was one of the reasons why I——"

"Went through a form of marriage with her."

"Why I thought I had married her." Julian made the correction very gently. "I did not think I should come back, Superintendent."

To my surprise, McNaught seemed to understand

him much better than I did. He raised his head, and his expression was deeply sympathetic. "I can understand a young chap's being wonderfully worried about who was going to look after his home, and the pack of good old servants his mother had died and left him with," he said unexpectedly, "especially if he'd known them from his childhood. I was in the last dust-up myself, and I know how one's got to go off and leave it. A fellow does the daftest things to try to keep it safe while he's away."

Julian met his eyes and grimaced wryly. "You're very shrewd," he said.

"It's my job to be so, sir." McNaught was happily sententious again. It was impossible not to like him. "Well," he said, "as I see it, Mrs. Phoebus saw her way to 'marrying' a young officer, to whom she had presented herself as an intelligent, responsible woman. Just the person to take care of his old dependents, and almost immediately after the ceremony he went overseas."

"Leaving her in complete charge," said Julian drily.

"Not quite, sir," McNaught corrected him quickly. "Don't underestimate your attorney. The Phoebuses might have stripped you but for him. He summed up Mrs. Rita very early on, and he forced her to keep the staff and the house going. She did herself as well as she could, I don't doubt, and Phoebus flourished likewise, but they couldn't do any real harm. He took care of that."

"I'm eternally grateful to him," said Julian fervently, "but I don't understand why they continued with this entrepreneur business. After all, they had all the money they needed."

"Very likely, but they hadn't the friends," McNaught explained. "Rita Phoebus was a woman who had to live in a crowd. Parties were the breath of life to her. So Phoebus carried on with his old tricks and drew a congenial set about them in no time. All was plain sailing until you came home. You were a sick man, but you were recovering rapidly. The rackety crowd began to avoid the house. Things weren't so good."

"And so they thought of killing me," said Julian bluntly.

"Yes," McNaught said shortly, and we sat in silence for a moment. Despite the fire blazing at my side, I felt the room had grown icy cold. Rita had so nearly succeeded.

"All the same," McNaught went on, "all the same, it was a considerable undertaking for them. They were confidence tricksters and blackmailers, but murder was something they hadn't attempted. To be honest, I think the woman got the idea only when she discovered the morphia where old Harriet had hidden it in the cupboard under the bookcase. Mrs. Rita must have found it the day she replaced the old lady's china with her cocktail paraphernalia. They tell me in the kitchen that she did that with her own hands."

"But how did she know it was morphia? It wasn't on the label," I put in.

"Oh, I'm open to bet that Phoebus knows morphia when he sees it," he said dourly. "It was remarkably like the luminal and came from the same dispensary in the same kind of bottle. She noticed that, and she realised how simple it would be to make a mistake."

"Why didn't she do it herself?" It was my question again.

McNaught turned to me, his eyes wide. "She knew she never could stand up to the enquiry, miss," he said promptly. "She knew there was bound to be a great deal of investigation, followed by an inquest. That was inevitable, and once the police started going into her motives, there was bound to be the very devil to pay. No, that wouldn't do at all."

"So she got hold of Gillie to—— My God, Superintendent, that's horrible!" Julian was bending forward in his chair, the knuckles of his clenched hands white.

"Yes, sir," said McNaught quietly. "She got hold of Miss Brayton. In fact, she did what ladies often do when there's dirty work to be done—she got a girl in. She was very clever, though; she found just the right girl. She chose an obviously innocent youngster who had no relatives to make a bother afterward, and one, moreover, who had a reputation already for being a little absent-minded. Just the type of girl, in fact, who would appeal to a coroner as one likely to make a silly mistake." He paused and grinned at me. "The staff at Totham Abbey was very helpful. I sent a man down there this morning after the doctor had told me his little bit."

"Oh," I said, my mouth dry.

"The doctor played into her hands all along," he observed. "He's an honest old chap, but not overburdened with brains. His brother seems to have held the practice together. She fooled him completely; he was all ready to believe anything she told him. He was certain you had made a mistake and confused the bottles, whereas, of course, what really happened was that someone confused the trays or the cups."

"But I didn't do that," I said.

"Didn't you?" He eyed me, his head on one side. "Maybe you didn't. Maybe Rudkin did. He tells me he's colour-blind, and I don't see why I should disbelieve him. The two shades are confusing by artificial light, anyway. That's what you discovered this afternoon, didn't you?"

"Yes," I said. "I didn't notice it last night, though."

"Perhaps not," he agreed. "Let's say Rudkin confused the trays, or that you, since you were crying, did not notice on which tray was the cup you put the tablets in. Besides, suppose you had noticed it, would it have mattered?"

"I don't understand," I said woodenly.

He looked at me curiously. "It was only a question of a sedative, wasn't it?" he said. "The sedative would hardly have hurt Mrs. Fayre after an exhibition of temper that, by all accounts, was something sensational." He sighed contentedly and lay back in the chair. "It's all fairly clear to you now, isn't it? The Phoebuses had had their plan made for some time, but Mrs. Rita did not put it into execution until you forced her hand."

"By telling her I was going?"

"Exactly. You took her by surprise, and with typical recklessness she decided to work at once. She had not much to do, but it needed a certain ruthless courage. Her idea was to open the pantry door with a second key, which she had had made for the purpose, change the tablet bottle, tamper with the light, and then wait. I wondered at first if the woman Mitzi had helped her there, but I'm inclined to doubt it. Mitzi had been with her for years; but, all the same, I don't think Mrs. Rita would have trusted her to that extent. At any rate, the Austrian didn't know where the cupboard was. She's been looking for something all day."

I was frowning. A small point was bothering me. "How could any coroner have thought I'd confused the bottles if there was only the morphia there?"

"Good girl," he applauded me. "You see, she intended to go back. I'm certain of it. She intended to return to the pantry during the night to restore the light and the luminal. She dared not leave it there in the first place, in case you noticed there were two bottles instead of one. In that case, you'd have read the labels, chosen the right one, and enquired about the other. Wouldn't you?"

"Yes, naturally."

"Of course. She knew that. So she intended to put it back afterward." He was very happy unravelling all the knots. "Then when the police arrived next morning, she could swear blithely that the two bottles had been there all these weeks," he continued triumphantly. "She could even afford to be frank, admitting openly that she had found the morphia herself and, not knowing what it was, had put it in the pantry long before you arrived here at all or even the Colonel came home."

"I should have denied that."

"Of course," he said. "But who would have believed you? You would have looked like a frightened schoolgirl who was trying to conceal her carelessness. There would have been a very unpleasant inquest."

He was right, I knew it. I could see it all happening

just as he described. I should have been utterly helpless, and Rita would just have shaken her head at me
and told me I'd broken her heart.

"You both have to thank your lucky stars for her grace
note," McNaught continued ominously. "If she hadn't
decided to make herself doubly safe by drinking some
of the coffee, she would have succeeded. I should be
sitting here cautioning Miss Brayton against negligence,
reproving her for lying, and"—he cleared his throat—
"we should have been alone."

"Since I should be dead," said Julian.

"Yes, sir," agreed McNaught quietly. "You underesti-
mated her all along, if I may say so. You imputed a bad
motive to her for getting this young lady into the house,
but you didn't choose one bad enough. She took the
coffee to prove she had perfect faith in Miss Brayton's
efficiency just in case she was ever questioned. There's
irony there."

I got up. "But all the same, I did it," I said. "I killed
her."

"Wait." McNaught was scratching his ear. "There's
just one little doubt about that. I ought not to mention
it, because I never shall be able to prove it; but for your
conscience' sake, Miss Brayton, consider Rudkin."

"Rudkin?"

He did not look at me. "Rudkin is a wise old man. I
doubt if much gets by him." He lowered his voice,
although we were alone. "Suppose," he began, "only
suppose, mind you, that Rudkin guessed something of
the sort was afoot. That light bulb must have made him
think, you know, although it made no impression on
you. Suppose he saw the two cups there waiting, and it
came into his mind that it might be a good idea to
change them."

We gaped at him, half guessing what was coming.

"If he was wrong," murmured McNaught, "there was
no harm done. Mrs. Fayre simply would take a sedative, which, after the way she'd been behaving, could
only have done her good. On the other hand, it was

quite possible that it would not hurt the Colonel to do
without his medicine for once. All this is only if Rudkin
was wrong in his suspicions. If he was right——"
McNaught paused. "Then it was criminal of him," he
said. "But no one's ever to know, are they? I don't
suppose he'll talk."

We were silent for a long time after that, and even
later, when McNaught had taken his leave, we said
little.

Stinker was snoring in his basket. Mrs. Munsen and
her brother were making themselves tea in the kitchen,
and the homely clatter of china reached us faintly in the
quiet house. Julian and I remained where we were by
the dying fire.

Presently I told him I was going back to my London
boardinghouse.

He did not misunderstand me, but glanced at me, his
eyes looking steadily into mine.

"For how long, Gillie?" he asked.

# Last Act

# ONE

She was running along in the rain. Her high heels clicked and skidded on pavement slabs as brown and clear as licked toffee and she bent her yellow head, in its gay green felt, against the gusts.

The message left for her at Victor's hotel had simply announced briefly that he had "already left." It was just like Victor to scuttle down to Zoff to get his story in first. She pressed on, the exasperating wind wrapping her narrow skirt round her slender knees, and blessed a suburb which appeared to possess no taxicabs.

It was nearly dark and the street lamps were coming out one by one. This was the old part of Bridgewyck which still retained some of the smugly sedate qualities of the market town it had been before a tidal wave of expansion had passed over it and joined it to the great city less than fifteen miles away. The wide street was lined with dark gardens, behind which solid family houses lurked amid secretive trees.

Margot Robert, white hope of the newly reformed Théâtre de Beaux Arts de Paris et Londres, was in no mood to admire them. She was becoming very wet. There were dark patches on the grey cloth of her suit and the leather sides of her week-end case glistened like running water when the light caught them.

The light caught her face, too, occasionally, and when it did hurrying passers-by turned despite the rain to look back after her.

Just recently intelligent folk in three capitals had been arguing about this young actress whose tragic

mother had been a stage star in the forgotten days of the
first World War, but whatever else was said of her, no
one ever suggested that she was not beautiful. At
twenty-four she had all the unlikely loveliness of a
Fragonard painting. She was slender, porcelain-fine and
pastel-coloured, a sunflower blonde with speedwell eyes.
So much was unanswerable, and one could take it or
leave it as one's taste decreed. But there the classic
china-doll effect ended abruptly. The last few years had
implanted character in the porcelain. There was a firmness
in the pointed chin, and the mouth, soft and primly
formed as a child's, could smile but never simper.
There was courage there, too, and intelligence, attri-
butes old Monsieur Fragonard would never have toler-
ated in a model.

Maurice Odette, the dramatic critic, writing in New
York a few weeks since, had protested plaintively that
"such a face should surely never hide a mind," but all
the same he had come waddling across the Stork Club
to say something kind at the party on the evening
before the company sailed.

However, she was not thinking of these triumphs as
she turned in at last through a pair of tall iron gates.
She was preoccupied with Zoff. Zoff's reactions had a
habit of mattering.

A gravel carriage drive lined with dripping laurels led
her to a monstrosity of a porch. This curious structure,
considered the most elegant thing in the eighties, was a
coloured glass conservatory big as a shop front and
domed like a temple, built to lie across the front door
and at least two of the windows. It was crowded with
palms and geraniums and smelled faintly medical. The
girl smiled as she entered its dimly lit warmth and
paused to tug the old-fashioned bellpull. The whole
house was so absurdly like Zoff. When Sir Kit had
offered to lend it to his old friend once the storm had
broken in Europe, he must, she felt, have realised how
exactly it would suit the famous *doyenne* of the French
stage whose career had been one of the more colourful

stories of the great era immediately before the wars.

The house was Zoff's period incarnate. The ridiculous palms and the solid comfort, the ormolu and the inch-deep carpets, the mock Gothic and the draughtproof doors, together they epitomised the world she had graced and scandalised and which was now as lost as only yesterday can be.

All the same, whatever else had gone, Zoff herself remained. Margot had heard her strong voice on the telephone that afternoon and was grateful for it. In a wavering world Zoff's famous temperament still repre-sented a constant if eruptive force.

The door opened slowly at first and then with a rush as Genevieve, browner than ever and if possible even more fat, appeared on the threshold, the warmth and colour of the overcrowded vestibule spread out like a back cloth behind her.

"Margot! *Chérie!*" She drew the girl in and hugged her in arms as strong as a navvy's, uttering all the time shrill parrot cries of protest at her wet clothes, com-mands that she change her shoes, enquiries, endear-ments, all the strident noises of her love and welcome.

Forty years in Zoff's somewhat exacting service had not altered Genevieve. She was still a Provençal peas-ant, outspoken, obstinate and indefatigable. Everything perturbed her for a moment and nothing for any length of time. She made a broad, sombre figure in her neat black dress and small black headshawl, but her huge hands were kind and there was an innocent merriness in her small black eyes like the merriness one some-times sees in the eyes of elderly nuns.

To Margot she was home. Twenty-three years before, Zoff had made one of her great gestures. At the first news of Marthe Robert's tragic death from an overdose of veronal she had driven to her young rival's apartment and had taken the weeping year-old baby in her arms, carrying her down to the carriage herself while the child wept wearily into her furs. After that, of course, she had passed Margot to Genevieve, and it was she whom the girl best remembered. Genevieve had bounced her on featherbed knees and had murmured funny old Provençal rhymes in her ears until she slept. In the morning it was Genevieve who waked, washed and fed her, kissed and scolded her and in the end made her forget; so now, in spite of everything, it was Genevieve and not Zoff who was *Maman* to Margot.

The old woman was overjoyed to see her darling.

"So it was a great success, this little tour, was it?" she demanded. "*Succès fou?* Ah, you can't tell me about that America. The times we had there, Madame and I, before you were born! We went all over the country, from one end to the other. When they couldn't photograph Madame they photographed me. You must go up at once and tell her, she will be so pleased. She needs pleasing these days. She's always so tired now. That does not suit her, you know."

Tired? Zoff tired? It sounded unlikely. In Madame Mathilde Zoffany's immediate circle it was usually everybody else who suffered that disability.

Margot looked worried. "I'll go now," she said, and then after a pause, "Is Victor here?"

Steps sounded on the landing above as the words left her lips, and they both turned a little guiltily as a man came gracefully down the stairs, bouncing a little on his toes, his shoes twinkling. Graceful, elegant, *soigné*, they were all words which suited Victor Soubise, and but for the faintly sagging curves under his cheeks handsome might have fitted him also. He came over to Margot at once and took her hand. Zoff's elder grandson had none of that remarkable woman's energy, but there was considerable charm in his narrow-lipped mouth and heavily lidded eyes. At the moment he appeared pleased with himself. There was a cat-and-cream-jug smugness under the long Norman nose. Margot ignored his welcome.

"You've been talking to Zoff."

He smiled at her disarmingly. "Naturally. After our discussion at dinner last night I thought perhaps I should." He had a light, affable voice and was unruffled as usual. He sounded eminently reasonable.

"Is—is she angry?"

"Darling!" He burst out laughing. "You look about fourteen, do you know that? No, of course not. Our *chère maîtresse* is sympathetic. She has been telling me that all great actresses are difficult to their fiancés. I have been hearing a great deal of ancient history."

Margot shrugged her shoulders. She was not smiling and her eyes had become a shade darker.

"You haven't been terribly clever, Victor. I shan't forgive you."

"I'm sorry." He made a deprecating gesture. "I assumed you would come down this morning. Denis is due tonight. You knew that, of course?" He glanced at her sharply and noted with satisfaction that her face grew blank, while Genevieve, who had stood listening to the conversation, uttered an indignant cluck at the name. Denis Cotton, only son of Zoff's elder daughter now dead, was not often mentioned in the household. Zoff disliked him for his mother's sake.

"No, I had no idea." Margot looked from one to the other of them in astonishment.

Victor laughed. "You've been away six months and you're out of the picture, my dear," he said. "In your absence Denis has been visiting, with some rather interesting consequences, or so it appears. Which reminds me, I shouldn't go into the drawing room if I were you."

"That is naughty." Genevieve turned on him as if he were still a child. "She has only just arrived, she is wringing wet and she has not yet seen Madame. No, that is abominable. Leave her alone. She will hear everything soon enough."

Margot began to laugh. Genevieve scolding and Victor telling tales, this was Zoff's household as everyone knew it. She put an arm round the old woman's shoulders and hugged her.

"What is in the drawing room, Gen'vieve? Tell me, or shall I go and look?"

91

Genevieve put up a hand to imprison hers in a grip like a trap.

"Be quiet," she murmured. "The doors in this house are not too thick. Sir Christopher Perrins is there."

"Sir Kit? Why didn't you tell me? I meant to go over to his house tomorrow. I'll just put my head in."

"No." The grip tightened. "Not yet. Not for a little while. He has the *juge d'instruction* with him."

"She means an inspector," said Victor casually. "A British inspector of police, very impressive, and about as useful as a circus horse in the circumstances."

Margot met his eyes and grimaced sympathetically. In most households the police are sufficiently uncommon visitors to cause a certain excitement in the family circle, but Zoff had never been a respecter of the minor conventions. In the course of her career she had sent for the police many hundreds of times. In earlier days the Prefecture had kept a special file for her complaints and a special officer to hear her troubles, and she had repaid the courtesy by performing at concerts in aid of police charities. It had been a most amicable arrangement.

"The jewels again, I suppose?" Margot spoke lightly, and before Victor could reply Genevieve came out strongly, her accent broad and convincing.

"That sort of thing. It is nothing, nothing at all." Then she scowled at Victor, who smiled over her head at Margot.

"The subject has been changed," he said. "Look, my dear, are you catching pneumonia before our eyes?"

"My God, yes!" Genevieve came back to practical matters with a rush. "You will come upstairs this instant, Margot. When you are dry you can come in to Madame. No, no more chatter, I forbid it. Come along, come along!"

She took the week-end case from Victor and, brushing him aside, seized the girl by the arm and propelled her firmly toward the staircase. Victor touched her hand as she passed.

"We meet at dinner, then," he said and turned away down the tiled passage.

The old woman glanced after him. "Now what is it?" she enquired.

"I'm not going to marry him. I told him last night."

"*Eh bien?*" Genevieve sounded unimpressed. She thrust the girl before her up the staircase. "These wars," she said breathlessly as they reached the top, "but for *les guerres* you would have been married these five years and Madame a great-grandmother. That is the trouble with these affiances, they do not keep well."

"I could hardly marry him when he was in Buenos Aires." Margot spoke defensively if indistinctly, as in the sanctuary of a bedroom her skirt was pulled relentlessly over her head.

"No?" agreed the old woman, panting from her exertions. "And if he were lying dead in a cellar after fighting for *la patrie*, you could not marry him either. Take off those knickers. They are wet also. Nonsense, I can feel them; they are damp also, I say."

A resigned and tousled Margot was clad only in a towel at the moment when the door opened. The bouquet of extravagantly unseasonable roses brought a waft of fragrance as it came slowly across the room, half hiding the figure who carried it.

The next moment there was a scream of amusement. The flowers flew away in a wide arc, leaving a shower of petals, as Zoff herself at her most boisterous threw out her arms.

"Darling, darling, darling! What are you doing? My God, we look like something from *Figaro*. I was going to make a speech in my best manner, the old actress salutes the young new star, and what happens? You spoil it all, you and that imbecile old woman. Standing about naked! My dear, how lovely you are and how *pink!*" She was laughing and crying and kissing and hugging, her years falling away from her like scattering hairpins, her eyes shining slits of black diamond in her dark skin.

Just for a moment Margot felt again the old childish
thrill of apprehension which this tempestuous personality had always engendered in her whenever they met
again after a little time. She loved Zoff, owed her
everything and admired her intensely, but she was still
a little afraid of her, even now when the great actress was
over seventy, and to touch her was to touch live wires.

As though she guessed something of the reaction, the
celebrity became comparatively quiet.

"Pretty little chit," she said, kissing her again to
smother her irritation. "How I love you. And I am glad
to see you, do you know. Margot, what a terrible
country this is, and what a horrible house. My God,
how I want to hear about somewhere else! How were
all my dear Americans? What did they tell you about me?"

"You're tiring yourself," Genevieve cut in as though
she were already halfway through an argument. "We
shall all pay for this. Why couldn't you wait in your
room until I brought her in to you? Look at all these
flowers! Completely wasted! Besides, if you can afford
flowers, why didn't you send a car to meet her? She's
wet to the shift." She waddled over to the roses as she
spoke and gathered them up, shaking them angrily into
some sort of order again. Zoff eyed her coldly and
seated herself upon the bed as on a throne.

"No taxi?" she enquired of Margot in bright, impersonal surprise. "What did I tell you? A terrible country!
It is typical. *Ma foi*, what a nation!"

In repose Zoff was not, and never had been, beautiful. She was a big-boned woman, not overtall, with a
shrewd, bold face whose wide mouth and narrow eyes
accentuated its character. Her visual charm lay in her
grace, which was amazing. It transformed every movement and made lovely every pose. The rest was vitality.
Even now, when her lips were blue under her dark
lipstick and her shock of hair was no longer gold but
white and dry as linen, energy flowed from her in a
stream. When she laughed, which was often, her eyes
gave off little dark sparks.

"Cheerful," she said with superb disgust. "Do you know, *chérie*, the people here are always cheerful. It is a virtue here. *Mon Dieu*, I can't understand it! They wear hair shirts and go up and down smiling bravely, too polite to scratch. They are disgusting. For myself, I shall obviously die here. You mustn't tell Kit that. The old villain wants to turn me out of his horrible dirty little house when I can no longer travel. He is a monster, that one."

Margot bent over the clean stockings Genevieve had produced and hid her smile. So this was the new persecution. One of Zoff's great virtues was openness. One was never mystified by her grievances. They came and went, but not in festering secret. The family technique had become adroit, however, and Margot changed the subject.

"I wore the headdress," she said.

"In *Phèdre*?" Zoff was beguiled. "You are too tall, of course," she said quickly. "You would dwarf it. But I expect it gave you a little courage, eh? What was this new play, *L'Amant*? Very dramatic? No? You shall read it to me when I am not so tired, and I shall show you how it should be done, perhaps. I am very ill. Do you know that? Did Gen'vieve tell you? The doctor here, who is a complete fool, says one day I shall die."

"So shall we all, God be praised," said Genevieve, who was still sulky. "The poor man said you should be quiet."

"Quiet?" The deep voice rose in a schooled crescendo. "How can I be anything but quiet in this absurd provincial back yard? I am being buried alive when I am not being actively murdered——"

"*Tiens!*" cut in Genevieve. "The poor child . . ."

"Of course." Zoff was penitent. "My poor little Margot, half drowned already, she does not want to hear about the old and the sick and hideous. No, we must talk about her." She paused reflectively and the mischievous black eyes became thoughtful. Margot climbed into a slip and smoothed the silk over her slender flanks. She

was waiting, listening intently, her white-gold curls
wild on the top of her head, her chin determined.

Zoff considered her, apparently dispassionately, and,
cocking her chin back suddenly, spoke over her shoulder.

"See those bones, Gen'vieve, those shadows there,
blue in the white back. Mine were never so good, never.
Not at my first confession. I had to make my way
without much beauty. Still, it is a great deal. Even now
when one knows how little it counts it takes one by the
throat. You shall have a dark dress, *petite*, with no back
at all. None, down to your little tail."

The voice ceased only for an instant. Almost without
break she added briefly:

"So my poor grandson Victor Soubise is not now
sufficiently exalted for the talented Mademoiselle Robert?"

"Oh, Zoff!" Margot swung round, the colour pouring
into her face. This was Zoff at her naughtiest, unfair and
enjoying it. "Don't, darling. Don't go and take it like
that. I wanted to talk it over with you. It never occurred to me that Victor would come roaring to you
before I could get here."

"Why should he not?" Zoff was playing the matriarch,
looking the part and not entirely acting. Behind her
were many generations of small landowners in the *Sud*
and she was dealing now with a problem which would
have been perfectly understood by any one of them.
"Your marriage to Victor has been arranged since you
were fifteen," she said. "It is only the wretched accident of war which has kept you apart in these important
years. It is a serious family business. There is property
to consider."

There it was, of course. Zoff had placed a finger on a
vital spot. As she said, there was a great deal of
property to consider.

As she was fond of pointing out, other actresses
acquired other things. Sarah Bernhardt preferred lions,
for instance. But Zoff had concentrated always on property, and now, even though France had been occupied
twice in a generation, much of it remained.

To begin with there was almost the whole of the famous Cap d'Azur, midway between Nice and Marseilles. Both Zoff and Genevieve had been born there when the place had been no more than a hamlet, but when she had inherited the estate which covered the shore line she had not sold it but put money into its development and had used her friends to make it fashionable.

During the brief glory of her second marriage, to Mégard, the perfume king, that time, money had poured into her ventures, and even after the occupation her faithful old notary could write very optimistically of leases and ground rents.

The Cap was by no means all the real estate. There was the block of luxury apartments in Paris which she had converted herself out of the mansion in the Rue de St. Anne. It had been her widow's portion from her first husband, that same Conte d'Hiver whose memory she had so abused in the famous *cause célèbre* which had shocked all Paris and nearly cost her her popularity.

Then there was the super-hotel in Lyons which she had bought for a song in the scare of '17, and the quay and the warehouses at Port Marius inherited from her own grandmother, the redoubtable Mère Zoffany of fabulous memory.

Lastly there were the two fine vineyards in the Rhône, the deeds of which poor Lampre, the great turf accountant, was said to have sent her from his death-bed. They were hidden in the straw of a champagne bottle, so it was said, and so passed unnoticed through a ravening multitude of creditors who swarmed over the anterooms in his fine house.

All these were still flourishing, all paying dividends. Zoff had picked her agents with genius and had had a flair for holding on at the right time. Also, of course, there were the jewels. Certainly there was property to consider.

Margot stood looking at Zoff now, following the train of thought behind the narrow forehead. The old woman was thinking of her possessions and what was to become of them.

In this matter she was not so free as one might have thought. Under French law there is no nonsense about disinheriting one's relatives. In France, if the children must inherit their parents' sins to the third and fourth generation, they do at least receive their property also.

Everybody knew how Zoff's fortune must be disposed. She had only two direct descendants, two grandsons. These were the cousins Victor and Denis, sons of her two daughters, one by each of her marriages.

Therefore, by the law of the land, each grandson must receive a full third of the whole of the estate, and only the remaining third was free. This last portion was settled on Margot, save for certain sums left to Genevieve and other dependents. It was all very simple and utterly inescapable. And yet, like many others who have built up fortunes by unswerving personal effort, Zoff recoiled from dividing hers. She had seen its power grow, had nearly lost it twice to the Boches, and now again felt the thrill of holding it. To her it was a living thing.

For its sake the marriage between Margot and Victor had been planned when the boy was in the schoolroom and the girl in the nursery. Denis, the other grandson, remained. Even Zoff had discovered there was no way round Denis.

Certainly she had done her best. The scandalous case which she brought in the French courts after her quarrel with her elder daughter, the sickly Elise d'Hiver, had almost cost her her career. The suggestion that a mother could get up in open court and swear that the baby she had carried in her arms at the famous reception when her secret marriage to d'Hiver was first announced was not her own child was too much even for the most delirious of fans.

Zoff lost and retired for a time. Elise died in childbirth after her marriage to a penniless American soldier of the first World War. But even after he too had lost his life in Picardy there was still the baby, still Denis.

The boy had been a thorn in Zoff's side all his life. He

had been brought up by servants on the small portion his mother had received from her father, and he had no help from Zoff.

Even this new war had not obliterated him. He had taken part in the resistance movement and, a second-year medical student, he had worked underground attending to the wounds of men fighting the invader. After a dozen hairbreadth escapes Denis remained.

At this very moment he was finishing his training in a London hospital, studying to take the final degrees he had not had time to acquire before the terror swept over the land again. When Zoff died, one third of her fortune must be his. There was no avoiding it. One third at least must be whittled off the whole, and now she was being asked to divide again.

All this Margot followed perfectly as she stood in the big bedroom looking thoughtfully at the old woman. She felt the situation was archaic. It was exasperating, belonging to an older world, but there it was, it was true.

"Oh, darling," she said, "I'm so sorry. Do, oh, do understand."

Zoff tilted her chin. It was a characteristic movement, curiously resourceful.

"You have decided against Victor, utterly?"

"Yes—that is, only, of course, that I don't want to marry him."

"*Eh bien*. This change in your heart, it had taken place on your trip to New York, yes?"

"No, not exactly. I decided finally on my way back, on board. But I've been thinking of it for some time, ever since I first saw Victor again when he got back from South America. How long is that?—six months at least." She was speaking earnestly but with caution. It was happening in the worst possible way. Zoff was forewarned and forearmed, and her personality was a force one had to fight against all the time.

"You took a dislike to Victor? You thought him changed? He was not a hero, he had not fought. Was that it?" The black eyes were penetrating and Margot looked away. It was not going to be possible to explain to Zoff that a man who had seemed a thrilling mystery of graceful sophistication to a girl of eighteen had become a rather spiteful old-ladyish bachelor in the eyes of an experienced woman of twenty-four. Zoff would not be interested in any such revelation. Her retort might easily be that a husband was not a lover, and what did one expect. Zoff still lived in an older France. Margot sighed and returned to the battle.

"Victor does not love me, and I don't love him," she said. "We never have, except as brother and sister. That won't do for marriage, Zoff, not nowadays. Don't worry about the property, my dear. Let him have my share as well as his own. You're free to give it to him. I'm not a relative. You've done everything for me and I'm more than grateful. I owe you everything and I love you, but I don't want any more. I'll be all right, Zoff. Don't worry about me. Count me out."

Genevieve had come up behind the bed, and now both the old faces, which were alike only in their expressions, were lifted anxiously toward the young one. Absently Zoff put up her hand and touched Genevieve's, which lay on her shoulder. She spoke for them both.

"Margot," she said, "there is one thing that we must know at once, *immédiatement*, now. Who is this man?"

"The man?"

"Yes, *ma chère*, the man. The man you have decided to marry instead of Victor. What is his name?"

Margot began to laugh. "Idiots!" she said. "Of course there isn't anybody. I should have told you at once."

"No one?" Zoff's eyebrows looked like circumflex accents. "I hope you are not unnatural," she said devastatingly. "No, of course not; it is one of those enormous Americans, more rich than I am, perhaps. Take no notice of him. Forget him. He will take you out of Europe. You'll never see your home again."

"Zoff, don't be absurd. This is the truth. There is nobody."

Zoff sniffed noisily and unromantically. She got up and put her arm through Margot's.

"Perhaps she's not such a bad vedette after all, eh, Gen'vieve? A very pretty ingénue performance, *chérie*. Come with me and see what I have done to make this miserable kennel habitable. Poor Kit is so angry with me. I have bribed an old bricklayer to help me to go round the bestial restrictions with which this infantile country surrounds itself, and I have thrown all the three front bedrooms into one grand salon. It is not good, but it is better than being stifled.",

"She has ruined the house," remarked Genevieve placidly. "Sir Kit has been *galant,* but the tears came into his poor eyes when he saw it. Run along. I will bring you a dress and you can do your hair in there."

Margot was not deceived. This brilliant digressing was one of Zoff's favourite manoeuvers. She would return to the main subject the moment Margot's own guard came down. All the same, the alterations sounded startling, and proved to be so when they crossed the hall to see the room. She had done just what she said. Two walls had come down and now the whole front of the house was transformed into one enormous apartment, in which Zoff's own huge rococo bed was almost lost. It was impressive but, for anyone but the *chère maîtresse,* utterly impracticable.

"The others," said Zoff magnificently, "sleep elsewhere. There are little rooms downstairs and attics also. Quite comfortable, I believe. I have not been up there because of my poor heart. Do you like it?"

"It's amazing," said Margot truthfully. "Extraordinary, darling. Can they keep it warm?"

"Seventy feet long exactly." Zoff spoke with satisfaction. "I take my exercise, walking once up and once down. By putting the mirrors at each end I feel I am going further. You don't like it, you silly little bourgeoise."

"I do, in a way. I don't think it was necessary."

101

"That is what Kit said. That man has a mean soul. He wants me to leave here because his son, who is a general coming home from the East, wishes to live in it with his hideous wife and children. I am beset by everybody. Margot, tell me, tell me quickly, is it Denis?"

The final question was a gentle hiss, loud enough to fill a theatre, and the strong fingers sank into the girl's forearm.

Although she had been waiting for the attack, the suddenness of it took Margot by surprise. She stiffened.

"Denis?"

"Yes, this man you intend to marry. Is it Denis?"

"Zoff, you're mad. Of course not. Denis doesn't want to marry anybody. Haven't you seen him, darling? He's a fanatic. He's crazy about his work. He'll never have time for marriage."

Zoff grunted. "I have seen him," she said with curious bitterness. "Since he has been in London he has become the dutiful grandson. At any rate, he has come to see me twice. As you say, he is fanatical." She paused and added casually: "But I hear that you have seen him. You have dined with him."

"Yes, twice, before I left for the States. He came to the theatre and took me out for a meal. He talked all the time about his work while we ate."

"In some filthy little *cabinet* of a restaurant, no doubt."

"Not a very grand place, no. He has no money, Zoff." To escape the catechism Margot took refuge in a question which had been worrying her. "Zoff, I know it's nothing to do with me, but do you pay Sir Kit for this house?" she said.

"*Pay* him?" The celebrity was aghast. "It is he who should pay me to live in the abominable ruin. Of course I do not pay him. I am his guest."

Margot hesitated. "I don't think he's very well off. The war has hit him badly, you know."

"*Tant pis.*" Zoff shrugged her shoulders. "We cannot help his troubles. He is very honoured to have me here. Poor Kit, he loved me very much once. Sometimes even now he loves me a little still. Do you find that disgusting?"

Margot blinked. Zoff really was a terror. Age seemed to be playing round her rather than touching her; just trying to get a word in edgeways, perhaps.

"Love is a very awkward thing," the great actress was apostrophising. "That is why these family marriages, which are all-important, should take place when one is very young. If one is young enough one can love anything. I expect that is why people cry when youth confronts them suddenly. It is envy." She cocked her head on one side and prodded the girl's shoulder with a long forefinger. "Should love arrive when one is older it is a different matter. To love is to become molten, you understand, and to pour one's self into a die. Afterwards, whatever one does, the pattern remains. If one escapes the first man, one loves again another exactly like him, and so on forever. It is very serious."

She seated herself in the high-backed gilt chair which had stood at the end of her bed ever since Margot could remember.

"You ate in a dirty *estaminet*," she observed, "and yet, *ma chère*, you went again to dine with Denis."

"Oh, leave Denis out of it!" In spite of her caution the young voice was raw, and Zoff's eyes flickered with sudden pain. Immediately her entire mood changed.

"As I get older I think too much and too quickly," she announced, "Poor *petite*, you will forgive old Zoff. She grows silly ideas as the other old women do. Now get yourself dressed. As for me, I must go down. I have a policeman to talk to." She got up slowly and moved over to the door, and for the first time it occurred to the girl that she had grown a little tottery. But on the threshold it was the old Zoff who looked back, mischief on her broad face. "I have to tell him I have made a stupid mistake," she said. "I wish I was your age. In that case, of course, it would be he who would have to apologise."

There was nothing ominous in her words, but as the door closed behind her Margot shivered. She sat down before the dressing table to do her hair.

## TWO

Sir Christopher Perrins walked sadly down the corridor. The house was his own but he hardly recognised it. Since Zoff had bedevilled it, the familiar atmosphere of sanctuary had disappeared altogether. The angry police inspector at his side was an anachronism if ever he met one.

In his youth Kit Perrins had been one of those happy little men whose round faces and smiling good humour sometimes deceive people into believing that they can have neither brains nor deep feelings. Both in the diplomatic and the elegant sporting circles which revolved round the great houses of those days he had been a great favourite without being a great figure. It was only afterward that his friends, looking back on him, realised how sound he had been, and also how nearly the tragic elements in his story must have touched him.

His marriage had been a miserable failure, but he never complained and no one heard of the bitterness brought into his life by the cold, greedy woman who had shared forty years of it. His fortune dwindled inevitably in the changing years, and a country never generous to the men on whom she relies had rewarded him hardly at all for a lifetime of service. Yet at seventy-odd—he was jocularly evasive about the "odd"—he remained a round and smiling person, old only by his wrinkles and a slight unsteadiness in his freckled hands.

At this instant he was deeply shocked. During his long friendship with Zoff she had provided him with plenty of awkward moments. For nearly fifty years she had retained her ability to startle the wits out of him, and on rarer occasions to scandalise his sophisticated soul. Today she had done it again. His round brown eyes were reproachful. This final scene, which had taken place not ten minutes before when she had calmly rescinded all her dreadful accusations of the morning, this really had taken a deal of swallowing. He glanced up at the furious policeman who walked beside him.

"The French are volatile," he ventured.

"Old ladies are often difficult, you mean." Inspector Lee spoke bluntly. He was a big man, heavily built, with an intelligent face which normally wore a mild, not to say resigned, expression. But at the moment he was irritated beyond endurance and did not care if he showed it. Kit sighed. There were times when he half wished he had left Zoff to the Hun, but as always, in the next breath he was ashamed.

"In her own country Madame Zoffany has been a little queen for a great many years."

"Oh, I understand perfectly, sir." The inspector cut him short because he could not bear to hear any more of it. When the complaint had arrived at the station it had promised something interesting and it was exasperating to find this explanation. "I understand what you're telling me. She did it to annoy and now she's changed her mind. We often get that sort of thing, but usually," he added spitefully, "in a rather different walk of life. In the ordinary way, an old woman calls in a constable and hands him out a lot of nonsense, and he tells her to have a drop of hot comfort and sleep it off. I came round myself today because when we get a serious charge from this kind of address there's usually something in it." He paused and added heavily: "I think I can say that I've practically satisfied myself that there is nothing in it, but it's a very funny little incident, you will allow that."

"An unfortunate incident," corrected Sir Kit gently.

"Queer," persisted Lee, partly to get his own back. "It does make one wonder what her relations are with her grandsons, you know, and then——" He broke off abruptly. Margot had turned the corner and was coming toward them. She wore a dark blue dinner dress whose colour echoed her eyes and the effect was considerable.

Kit, who adored her and had been longing to see her, could have wished her anywhere else. She came forward, her hands outstretched.

"Here I am."

"Margot, my dear child!" Lee watched the embrace with gloomy interest.

"This is the adopted granddaughter, I suppose?" he said.

Kit frowned. The man was in the right and had a grievance, but he was taking advantage of the position.

"This is Mademoiselle Robert, Inspector," he said stiffly. "A young friend and heir of Madame Zoffany's. Margot, I shall be with you in a moment. It's good to see you, my dear. The trip doesn't seem to have hurt you, thank God."

It was on the tip of Lee's tongue to say that the young lady looked bonny wherever she had been, but he checked it. The girl looked human enough, but they were all alike, these people. When one of them created trouble they all crowded round and made a screen like players on a football ground round the man who has lost his shorts. Just as she was moving off, however, an idea occurred to him. As she passed him he turned on her.

"You're the young lady who made Madame Zoffany change her mind, are you?" At once he was aware of scoring. The girl looked startled but wary, and the old man coloured but recovered himself at once.

"You underestimate Madame Zoffany, Inspector," he said easily. "No one on earth has ever changed her mind for her. It—er—follows some weathercock law of its own, don't you know. Mademoiselle Robert has only just returned from a trip abroad and has not yet heard anything of the mistake which brought you here to-night. I was rather hoping she never would. And now, Inspector, there's nothing I can do but repeat my

106

sincere apologies. Margot, I think dinner has gone in. I'll join you in the dining room, my dear."

Lee recognized dismissal. Deep in that quiet voice of the old school lay a chorus of other voices, neither so soft nor so courteous, voices of lawyers, voices of magistrates, voices of high-ranking police officials addressing subordinates who had exceeded their duty. He gave in regretfully.

Margot smiled good-bye and went off down the corridor, leaving a breath of L'Heure Bleu behind her. Lee followed Sir Kit to the front door, where they parted amicably. But the inspector went out into the rain wondering if he had not perhaps stumbled on something after all. Had the old man been far too anxious for him not to question the girl? Lee could not be sure. The household would bear keeping in mind.

Sir Kit hurried back through the hall. He felt tired and heartily ashamed of the whole shocking business. It was not fair of Zoff, it really was not fair. He was very angry with her. He brightened a little as he entered the dining room. Of all corners of the house it had most nearly escaped the tenant's innovating hand. The worn Chinese wallpaper and austere late Georgian mahogany remained much as he remembered them as a child, and the atmosphere was warm and safe and polite still as it had been long ago when his aunt Birdwood, who had left him the house, had first entertained him at her luncheon table.

Victor and Margot were already seated when he came in, a place left empty for him between them. Evidently Zoff had decided not to appear. She seldom came down to dine these days, but Kit understood that she was keeping out of his way tonight. It was even just possible that she was a little ashamed of herself. He hoped so. At the same time he missed her. She might have come down, he thought, she might have come down. Margot was pleased to see him, that was some compensation. She was laughing across the room at him now and patting the chair beside her.

As usual, Felix was waiting on them. He had been in Zoff's service for something like thirty-five years and had never, by Sir Kit's standards, ventured within assessable distance of becoming a reasonable servant. He was an old man now, thin and slightly seedy, with greasy hair and depressed eyes. Kit said he was like a waiter in a boulevard café and in the early days had remonstrated with Zoff about him.

"But he never sleeps, *mon ami*," she had protested. "It is such an accomplishment."

So Felix had remained and here he was still, creeping about in black felt slippers, serving sloppily, and listening to the conversation without pretence. Tonight he did remember to pull out the chair, however, and Kit sat down gratefully to tepid soup and his dear Margot.

"I started," said Victor. "I hope you'll forgive me. I sat watching a slice of carrot congealing and I felt it or I should be put out of our misery. The Law has departed, has it?"

"At last." Kit scowled over his spoon. "An unfortunate business, safely concluded," he added with a finality calculated to silence even Victor. "Zoff given us anything to drink?"

Felix filled his glass with sherry. "Imported by the Government, m'sieu."

Kit received the bad news philosophically. "And then?"

"Then the Latour, m'sieu, since Mademoiselle has returned."

Kit's smile re-emerged and he dropped a hand over Margot's.

"So nice to see you, my dear," he said, meaning it. "Nice about the Latour too, eh? I cursed Zoff's baggage when she arrived, but I see her wisdom now. We had a furniture van to bring her trunks from the docks. The war had started too—— God bless my soul, I don't know how she did it."

"*Les pourboires.*" Fortunately Felix did not speak aloud, although his lips formed the words. Experience had taught him not to interject remarks when Sir Kit was at table, but he still made a token of doing so to prove to himself that he was not subservient. When Zoff noticed the manoeuver it amused her immensely.

"This may be the wrong moment, but I should like to hear——" Victor was beginning when Margot shook her head at him.

"The meal is special for me," she said. "We're having everything I like best, as far as it's possible these days. How's that for a welcome home?"

Victor shrugged his shoulders. "Have it your own way," he said irritatingly, "but I can't see that this is a thing we can laugh off. At least someone ought to warn Denis not to come here."

"My dear fellow"—Sir Kit passed a weary hand over his forehead—"My dear, dear fellow, not with the Latour, eh?"

"As you wish." Victor seemed determined to behave like a spoilt child. "I only feel you're making a dangerous mistake in taking it for granted that Zoff didn't realise quite what she was saying. I can't put it any plainer than that, can I?"

Sir Kit laid down his knife and fork. "Zoff has withdrawn her disgraceful accusation against Denis," he said slowly. "She has taken back every word of it in front of the police. Really, you know, I think we must leave it there."

"I heard about that from Gen'vieve. All the same, if Zoff ever believed——"

"Really, Victor." Sir Kit's fury was mounting dangerously. "I shall be obliged if you will let this disgraceful subject drop. Young Cotton has been slandered, actionably so, don't doubt that. The very least we can do is to be silent. Zoff must be out of her mind and Denis has my profound sympathy."

"That's very nice of you, Sir Kit." The voice from the doorway behind them was very deep. The tone was casual and friendly, but the actual timbre was characteristic and unforgettable. Margot swung round at it,

109

Victor was silenced, and the atmosphere of the room changed as a new force flowed into it.

"Denis, my dear fellow." Sir Kit placed his glass in safety and prepared to rise.

"Please don't, sir." The newcomer advanced to shake hands, the light from the candles on the table lending him an elegance which was not his by right. He was strong and compact, taller than Victor and a shade more heavily built. In face he bore no likeness whatever to his cousin. He was fair, with a firm, ugly jaw and grave, deep-set eyes, and he did not belong to Victor's world nor yet to Kit's. There was a modern utilitarian sturdiness about him which made them both look a little old-fashioned. "I'm sorry I'm late," he said, "but the trains were against me. Gen'vieve let me in and sent me straight here. Hallo, Margot. Hallo, Soubise. I'll come and sit over there by you, Victor, if I may—so I can look at you, Margot."

He was more at ease than any of them, and the most outstanding thing about him was a certain authority, as vigorous in its way as Zoff's own. They were all attracted to him and all resented it. The clash stimulated the conversation and yet constrained it, and the faint note of uneasiness, almost of danger, which had been sounding in the house ever since Margot entered it became more apparent as the meal progressed. Kit kept the ball rolling gallantly and Denis assisted him, but the other two were unusually silent. And yet it was on Felix that Denis had the most visible effect. For a time, at any rate, he waited almost well, exhibiting a most uncharacteristic deference. So Felix remembered a jaw and a voice like that also, did he? Sir Kit had forgotten the ruffian had been in service so many years.

With the ices came Zoff's second surprise for the homecomer, a bottle of pink champagne. It was far too sweet for Kit's taste, but the sight of it delighted him. For a minute or two it brought back to him a lost world which had been very lovely, so that there he was again in it with a beautiful girl laughing at him over a tall glass while little scented bubbles danced between them. He was suddenly so happy that he had forgotten the trials of the day, and it was with a wave of pure rage that he heard Victor breaking into the chatter.

"How much longer have you over here, Cotton?"

"At the hospital? About three weeks."

"And you go back at once after that?"

"Good heavens, yes!" The youngster was fervent. "I've been away too long already."

"Is there so much to do?" It was Margot. She was sitting up straight, watching him with eyes as darkly blue as the china of her plate.

"So much that I——" he began, and broke off laughing. "I told her," he said, turning to Kit. "I sat and told her until the waiters put the chairs on the café tables. I talked and talked until my voice gave out and she was white with exhaustion. There is a lot to do, of course. The upheaval has unleashed God knows what. It'll take a lifetime to get it under, and that means hurry."

He spoke without affectation, and Sir Kit warmed to him.

"I saw my old friend Anthony Watkin the other day," he remarked. "He tells me you're doing rather brilliantly at St. Mark's. That so?"

Denis coloured. "That was very handsome of him," he said. "I had a certain amount of experience with the Maquis, of course."

"You're a surgeon?"

"I hope to specialise on that side."

"Good luck to you," said Sir Kit, making the cliché heartfelt.

"Good luck to you, indeed," agreed Victor seriously. "As a life it sounds like hell to me. I don't think I could face Europe these days. People in the mass give me the horrors, even when they're not displaced. Three weeks, you say? Then you probably won't be coming down here again. I think that's wise." He spoke with apparent sincerity, and Denis turned in his chair.

"You mean that kindly, I hope?" he said, laughing.

"I do." Victor's heavy lids disappeared into his head, leaving his eyes unexpectedly disarming. "I do. I simply felt you ought to be told. And the others ought to realise it too. Zoff wouldn't do a really dreadful thing like this out of mere caprice. You don't know Zoff."

The final injustice was too much for Sir Kit, who all but choked. Margot intervened.

"Zoff's is a world of italics," she said. "Don't let's be muddled by it. I haven't gathered the exact details of the present excitement, but I suppose Zoff has been to the police again about her jewels. Isn't that it? And I suppose that this time she's mentioned Denis, because he's the newest arrival. It's very awkward, I know, but then it always is, isn't it? Zoff's jewellery has been the centre of family crises ever since we were children. Practically the first thing I remember is Zoff losing an emerald earring and accusing Gen'vieve of selling it to buy candles to coax a husband out of St. Catherine."

There was an uncomfortable silence as she finished, and even the clatter Felix made with the fruit plates sounded nervous. Denis drew a pattern with his forefinger in a patch of salt which had been spilled on the polished wood. When at last he looked up at her his smile was apologetic.

"My grandmother isn't very keen on me," he said, evidently attempting to make the statement as light as he could. "I'm afraid she feels I may be overanxious to inherit the money I need for my clinic in Caen, and when I told her I was coming down today she appealed for police protection. I'm afraid she thinks I may attempt to kill her. That's it, isn't it, Sir Kit?"

"Oh—oh dear," said Margot inadequately. "She couldn't have *meant* it. I mean, I've never known her do anything quite so dreadful as this. But she wouldn't really honestly mean it. Zoff—well, Zoff does do things."

"What did you say to her upstairs that made her change her mind?" Victor put the question curiously, his eyes on her face. They were all looking at her and she spread out her hands.

"Nothing. I didn't even know about it, you see. I only had ten minutes or so with her when I was changing." Her voice died away as the truth dawned on her with sudden brutality. Zoff *knew*. Of course. In some terrifying intuitive way of her own, Zoff had found out. As soon as Zoff had seen her she had known about the humiliating thing that had happened to her, the same thing which even now was tying up her tongue and playing exasperating tricks with her breath.

Zoff had not been surprised, that was one mercy. There was no folly in the whole repertoire of woman-kind which was unknown to Zoff. It would never have struck her as incomprehensible that a successful, sought-after young woman, experienced and sophisticated, should find herself helpless and unhappy because she could not forget even for an hour a fanatic with a pleasant voice whose heart was set on other things. Even the fact that this miracle should have happened after only two meetings would not have astonished Zoff. She would have seen it as a disaster but not an improbability.

Her first act had been typically practical. Immediately on the discovery she had withdrawn at once an accusation which was so outrageous that it must increase the young man's interestingness to any attracted eyes. Margot felt a stab of apprehension. Zoff was never discreet. It was bad enough to suffer this lovely cruelty without the knowledge that it was being discussed.

She crept guiltily out of her thoughts, to find Kit doing his best to save the ruin of a fine dinner.

"Felix," he was saying, "as the oldest guest present, I think I might tell you to go and find some of our hostess's Courvoisier."

"Madame said to serve the Napoleon tonight, m'sieu."

"Good heavens, has she still got some?" Sir Kit was startled out of all his troubles. "An amazing woman," he said reverently. "Well, well, Margot, my dear, you must come home again."

So Zoff had raised her little finger and twiddled poor Kit round it once more. Yet damage had been done.

The three young people were quiet and there was constraint between them, while the rain on the windows made angry little patches of sound in the long silences.

## THREE

The drawing room at Clough House, Bridgewyck, had been designed in a quiet age. Its white panelled walls were not very tall but in their time they had embraced with ease twenty couples at the polka, and they were hung with old colour engravings in delicate oval frames. Kit's aunt Birdwood had left her best walnut there and, dotted about on the flowered carpet like vast old ladies picnicking, were companies of wing armchairs with wide, hard seats and chintz petticoats half hiding their stout claw feet.

Into this prim haven Zoff had crammed her own more flamboyant treasures, and the effect was both disturbing and a mite exciting, as if Madame de Pompadour had come to tea with Jane Austen.

Felix served coffee there after dinner, another concession to Sir Kit, who enjoyed the small formality. There was a coal fire on the hearth, the faded silk curtains were drawn against the rain, and when Margot was safely settled behind the silver tray the old man came sauntering in, neat and happy, a cigar between his lips. She glanced up at him slyly and thought how charming he was and yet how pathetic, as he enjoyed so eagerly the little scraps of elegances left in a world from which the silver plate had almost worn away.

"They've gone out to look at Victor's car," he said, smiling down at her from his halo of blue smoke. "They'll be in in a moment. It's an extraordinary thing how young men always want to inspect the fashionable method of locomotion the moment they've been properly fed. In my days we always trotted out to look at each other's horses, the things truly nearest our hearts,

I suppose. Very interesting. You look very beautiful, my dear."

"Thank you, darling. Or isn't that right? What ought one to say to that remark? I never know."

"Nothing clever," he said promptly. "No sugar, my dear. Just the black coffee. Well, that passed off very well, considering, didn't you think? Denis behaved excellently, I thought."

Margot lay back in her chair, the deep blue of her dress enhancing the whiteness of her arms as they lay upon it.

"Not one of Zoff's jollier performances, though," she said at last.

"No," he agreed, "but still a Zoff. That made it all right, you know. It always has, and please God it always will. You were quite right when you said she lives her life in italics. She does, and everybody knows it, so it doesn't matter."

He sat down a little wearily and drew his chair closer to the fire.

"A dreadful accusation," he said. "Monstrous, of course. If anyone else had made it I don't know what one could have said about it. But you see, everybody recognizes Zoff's exaggerated temperament, if only subconsciously. No one took this seriously, not even the police." He sighed. "That's that, then," he said.

Margot was silent. She sat looking at the blue flames among the red coals and the forefront of her mind was busy, or attempting to be busy, with Zoff and Kit in an idle speculation on the kind of relationship which must once have existed between them to produce this simple fidelity in him. But in the back of her mind she knew that she was waiting, listening, hoping for Denis to come in. While resenting the fact bitterly, she could not escape from it. Once she fancied she did hear a step in the hall and her heart stirred roughly, disturbing her breath. She frowned and sat up impatiently.

"Kit, oughtn't we to get Zoff to go home to Cap d'Azur?"

115

"Eh?" He came out of his thoughts with a start. "I wish you would, my dear. I don't know how much she's said to you, but I admit I've gone so far as to suggest it. I'm in the devil of a position. This is my son's house. I made it over to him some years ago. Kind of a wedding present, as a matter of fact. Then the war came and he was kept in India and I offered it, with his consent, to Zoff for the duration. Now he's on his way home with a wife and young children and naturally he expects to live in it." He paused and shook his head. "She's not even happy here," he said sadly. "Between ourselves, she's been very dissatisfied. First it was the cooking arrangements. Then she said the place was infected with flies, and we saw to that. And now she thinks the rooms are too small. Yet she won't let me have her flown back to the South. She could be there in a few hours, you know. She's thinking about her luggage. There's a ton of it and she'd have to have it crated and sent on after her. She doesn't like that."

He glanced round the room and she followed his eyes. Zoff's belongings were everywhere, none of them looking particularly moveable. The Vincennes candelabras alone—each slender branch a mass of exquisite porcelain flowers—presented an alarming packing problem.

"Hullo, clock stopped." He got up and trotted across the room. "That won't do. Zoff's superstitious about things like that."

The clock was a great possession. It had been made by Jerome Martinot for Henry XIV and it stood over four feet high, a graceful if extravagant gesture in ormolu and buhl, with a bold enamel face and a gilt Father Time on its crest. The screws supporting its heavy bracket must have defaced Aunt Birdwood's pitch-pine panelling and its flamboyance made the Wheatleys pale, but taken by itself, it was a lovely thing. Zoff adored it. It had been given her by a king and she insisted on taking it with her everywhere she went, despite Genevieve's protests that she might more conveniently have adopted a steam roller as a mascot.

Margot sat watching Kit's precise back as he unlocked the case.

"All right?" she enquired.

"Margot, come here." His tone startled her and sent her over to him.

"What is it?" she demanded, and he stepped back to show her.

The hands of the clock were slender and finely wrought but they were made of iron and were very strong. And yet someone had forced them out of the true, wrenching the pins and twisting the points. Inside, the pendulum lay flat in the case, its shaft broken in two.

She stood staring at the damage, the senseless spite of it sending the colour out of her face. In this house, where so much had been talked of mock violence, this example of the genuine thing was startling. Someone had been considerably exerted to do wanton harm. In Aunt Birdwood's drawing room the discovery seemed blankly incredible.

"I can't believe it," she said.

"Touch the bell, will you, my dear?" Kit's head was still half in the clock.

Felix arrived after an interval. He came sidling round the door, openly reproachful at the extra journey, but when he saw the trouble his jaw dropped.

"*Sacré!*" he said and burst into a noisy flood of patois. "It is a portent, this. A bad omen. There is an enemy. Someone, some vandal, some unspeakable *sale cochon* has been in the house. We shall have serious trouble. Madame will be enraged. She must be told at once. Possibly it will kill her."

"All the more reason she should not be told." Kit spoke testily. "Don't make such an infernal noise, Felix. Don't be a fool, my man. Pull yourself together. Go and fetch Gen'vieve and—and no word to Madame. I never did like that fellow," he added as the door closed. "An unbalanced boor and a damned bad servant, in my opinion. A nasty business, this, Margot. Some wretched charwoman with a grievance, I suppose."

"A very strong charwoman." Margot spoke absently and found him staring at her. He opened his mouth to speak and changed his mind.

· He was holding the pendulum shaft and peering at the break through one glass of his pince-nez when Genevieve appeared with Felix behind her. She was furious; the very set of her head shawl betrayed it. Her sturdy figure advanced on the clock, her small eyes surveyed it, and then she faced them.

"*Mon Dieu*, Margot, you have only been back ten minutes and then this occurs. Madame will be beside herself."

Kit grimaced. "Neither myself nor Miss Margot are guilty," he said with that touch of superiority which always annoyed Genevieve. "You have some cleaner with a grudge against you, I'm afraid."

"There is no cleaner save myself." The old woman's French was as broad as her bosom. "Do you think I would permit one of these clumsy foreigners in here with Madame's priceless valuables? No! If I did, this is what I should expect. One of the household has done this. I know what Madame will say."

"But, Gen'vieve, that's ridiculous and it's also very rude." Margot's protest was firm. "Was the clock all right when you came in to light the fire?"

"Naturally it was. Poor Madame, this will set her off again on her terrors. I tell you, *petite*, I know what I know."

"They have no sense of insult." Sir Kit made the observation with infuriating detachment. "I've noticed it time and again. Gen'vieve, that will do. Not a word to Madame Zoffany. I'll get a man in at once and we'll get everything put right before she hears of it. We can go into the mystery later. The repairs are the main thing.

Meanwhile you must keep her out of this room if you can."

Some of the fury died out of Genevieve's eyes at this promise of escape from the storm she anticipated, but she was still flustered. "It will not be difficult," she said drily. "*Monsieur le docteur* is with her now."

"The doctor?"

"He was expected. It was arranged yesterday. Madame desires Mademoiselle to see him."

Kit glanced questioningly at Margot, but she shook her head.

"This is the first I've heard of it. I'll come up with you now, Gen'vieve. Kit, my dear, are you sure we can leave this to you? It seems a frightful imposition."

"Yes, yes, run along. I'll see to it. Don't tell Zoff."

Felix shuffled forward. "Madame will expect to know," he murmured, but wilted before the look that Kit gave him.

Genevieve touched the ormolu moulding with a caressing forefinger.

"*Quel dommage*," she said softly. "It is a horror, this, to happen to such an old friend. Come, mademoiselle."

Margot went after her. Why Zoff should have arranged for her to interview her doctor at this time of night she had no idea. It signified nothing, of course. In that house Zoff's whim was the only reason for everything.

A recollection occurred to her as she walked slowly up the stairs behind the panting old woman.

"I have to go to London tomorrow. There's a luncheon. It's being given for me. I'll be back in the evening."

"So much the better." Genevieve was breathing heavily. "It is not right that Madame should be alone with this young Cotton."

"That's idiotic, darling."

"Very well." Genevieve paused on the step to raise a crumpled, angry face. "See *monsieur le docteur*, and if Madame is mistaken, then tell me this: why does he come? Nobody wants him. Why does he come?"

Margot had nothing to say. The question had been there in her own mind.

"You see?" Genevieve was breathless. "It is quite possible that Madame is not being mistaken. It is possible that he has something in mind." She went on again, hauling her heavy body upward by the banisters. Once on the landing, she glanced round. "Ah," she said, "here is *monsieur le docteur* waiting. M'sieu, permit me, this is Mademoiselle Robert. Mademoiselle, *monsieur le docteur* Philip Ledbury."

Margot turned to meet Zoff's latest doctor. After years of experience she was prepared to find him of any variety, eminent, unknown or witch, yet the man who came smoothly toward her, his hand outstretched, was unexpected. He was young, and gravely good-looking in a way long since out of fashion. Sleek golden hair flowed back from his high forehead. Perfect features were covered with a milky skin, and the hand which touched hers was long and white and gentle. His aplomb was superb. He swooped down upon her and gathered her into his confidence in an instant.

"Oh, I'm so glad to meet you, Mademoiselle Robert. I wonder if we could go in here and talk for a moment? I don't know whose room it is. Oh, yours? Splendid. I just want a few words with you in private. You'll go in to Madame Zoffany, will you, Gen'vieve? You'll find her perfectly comfortable, I think. Just see she keeps the lights lowered tonight, won't you? I think she's been a little unwise to read and write by artificial light. That's all right, then. In here, Mademoiselle Robert."

He parted them and swept them into the two doors with the ease and energy of a sheep dog at the trials. He talked all the time, his voice brisk and persuasive, but he did not smile. Not even a polite curl disturbed the perfection of his mouth or lit the cold greyness of his eyes.

Margot went into the bedroom, and he followed her and seated himself upon the bed without apology.

"It's so difficult to speak frankly before servants,

however old and trusted, don't you think? I wonder if you'll smoke? You won't? Oh, splendid. But do if you'd rather." He put away his case with a little snap, drew up one knee, which he clasped, and surveyed her earnestly over it.

"Now I know you're not a grandchild," he began. "Zoff—she lets me call her Zoff, by the way, because she knew my grandfather in Vienna, which is rather sweet of her—well, Zoff has explained everything to me, and I saw at once, of course, that you were the person with whom I should have my little chat."

Margot nodded encouragingly. She had placed him now as a product of one of the older universities who for some family reason must have taken up medicine. His type abounded in the other professions. She sat down on the dressing stool.

"What do you want me to do?"

"Ah, you see that, do you? That's very good. Quite excellent. Sometimes relatives don't realise their responsibilities." He was still unsmiling, still clasping one long, thin shin. "Of course my sole interest is in my patient. You do understand that, don't you? I'm not in the least concerned with dear old Zoff's family affairs, but I am most desperately interested in her health."

"Naturally," she murmured, and he cocked an eyebrow at her and relaxed a little.

"At any rate, I'm convinced of one thing. She must not be allowed to see this young Maquis recruit of a grandson of hers again. As her doctor I forbid it. I can't put it plainer, can I?"

"I don't suppose you can," she said stiffly. Her first reaction was one of intense irritation. His airy reference to Denis's war service was distasteful. But her next thought was more disturbing. Surely no professional man would make a statement like this without good reason? Something must have been happening in this big, brightly lit house that she did not understand at all.

The doctor was still talking.

121

"I am relying on you to see that I am obeyed," he was saying. "They must not meet, either alone or with other people present. She is wonderfully strong constitutionally, but there's a definite heart murmur there and of course she's not young. The time has come when she must take care of herself."

Margot looked at him in astonishment. This description of Zoff's heart trouble was very different from the picture she had received from the woman herself.

"I thought she was seriously ill," she said.

"Seriously but not dangerously," he corrected her pedantically. "The actual condition is not alarming, or even unusual, in one of her age, but those two attacks were so extraordinary—and, if I may say so between ourselves, so significant—that I really must insist that every possible precaution is taken. I do hope I make myself clear."

"I don't think I know about the attacks." She was sitting up stiffly, her head a little on one side, her eyes alarmed. She looked very lovely and he warmed to her, betraying his youth in a sudden burst of confidence.

"Oh well, if they haven't told you, I can understand," he said. "It really is the oddest thing, and to be frank, I've never seen anything like it and I'd have pressed for another opinion if she hadn't made such a complete recovery. It's probably some kind of hysteria, although she's hardly that kind of subject, is she, d'you think?"

Margot shook her head.

"No," he agreed quickly. "Highly strung and temperamental, of course, but hardly hysterical. And yet, on the evidence, I can't account for it in any other way. I've not been her medical adviser for very long. She used to call in old Dr. Kay from Peter Street, and then found him rather unsympathetic, I'm afraid, and sent for me. I've been attending her for about three months now. She was going on perfectly well, I thought, and then one day a most extraordinary thing happened." He paused to fix Margot with his pale, unsmiling eyes. "Gen'vieve sent for me in a great state and I found

Madame in a very curious condition. She had been very excited and almost incoherent, Gen'vieve told me, and had then appeared to faint. She had come round by the time I arrived, and although there was evidence of some exhaustion, there was nothing to worry about. Gen'vieve had propped her up by an open window, and although I examined her thoroughly, I found very little amiss. Yet something had happened. Her story was that she had been talking to her grandson from the Maquis alone in the drawing room, and that after he left her she lost consciousness."

He hesitated.

"I could see she didn't like the man, of course," he said, "but she was semidelirious when Gen'vieve came in and she was alone then. I shouldn't have taken it very seriously if it hadn't happened again on his next visit. This alarms you, does it?"

Margot drew her glance from his face and got up.

"No," she said. "No, I don't think it does, not yet."

"Have you ever known anything like it to happen to her before?"

"No, I haven't, but—but are you sure, Doctor, that Mr. Cotton had anything to do with this at all?"

"Naturally I'm not, or I should have had to take some action." His voice ran on easily. He was enjoying it, she thought wryly.

"But he was in the house each time, and each time, significantly enough, he had just left her when the attack occurred."

"Was Denis there the second time?"

"Oh yes. Zoff was in her bedroom and Denis Cotton had gone in to say good-bye to her. Gen'vieve heard him leave the house and then went up to her mistress. She found her lying on her bed, her handkerchief pressed to her lips. She was practically unconscious. Fortunately Gen'vieve carried her to the window, drenched her with eau de cologne, and then had the sense to ring me. When I came, Zoff was weak but quite normal, save for a slight worsening of the heart condition and some nausea. She could tell me nothing, except—which seemed to me to be rather cogent, you know—that she did not remember Cotton going."

"I see." Margot spoke huskily. "Have you spoken to Denis?"

"I? Good heavens, no!" He seemed scandalised. "That's not my province. No, my duty is to protect my patient and then, if I am convinced that an attack is being made on her, to inform the police. I'm a doctor. I can't go interfering in anything that is not my direct concern. I did feel I should speak to someone other than a servant, though, and Zoff begged me to come this evening and see you. To be honest, I expected someone older."

He was still very self-possessed, still happy in his own importance.

"Do you think you can enforce my orders? She mustn't see him this time. If he's heard anything about it at all, I am amazed that he came again."

Margot ignored the final comment.

"No," she said slowly. "No, he mustn't see her. I do understand that. For both their sakes . . . It's a coincidence, of course, or else, as you say, some sort of hysterical seizure. Are you sure there was nothing else to explain it, Doctor?"

"I'm not infallible," he said with dignity, "but I've found nothing to account for it. On each occasion recovery was complete in twenty-four hours. I haven't made any official complaint, for the elementary reason that I've no evidence against anybody. However, should something else occur whilst Mr. Cotton was again in the house, well, the probability of it being another coincidence would be rather strained, wouldn't it?"

He was silent for an instant, but added almost immediately:

"Believe me, I know it's very awkward, but you do see the need for caution, I hope?"

"I do. You can rely on me," she agreed quietly. "It's some sort of nerve storm, of course, brought on by the sight of Denis, if that's possible. She's never liked him, you see. She quarrelled with his mother."

To her relief he knew the story.

"That was the elder daughter, of course?" he said. "The one there was the case about?"

She nodded and he sat looking at her earnestly.

"It's terribly fascinating, you know," he remarked unexpectedly, "especially in view of all the new work that has been done in the psychotherapeutic field lately. There's probably quite a fixation there—desperately interesting. We'll get Brogan or McPhail to see her later on. Meanwhile I'll leave it to you. I shall drop in tomorrow, probably in the afternoon, just to jolly her along."

He got up and moved over to the door, his golden head a good foot above her own. As he passed her he hesitated.

"In your opinion this Denis person couldn't possibly have done anything—stupid? Is that so?"

It was on the tip of her tongue to tell him that the very notion of it was ridiculous, but a thought checked her. Denis was a complete mystery to her. She believed with all her heart that he could do nothing that was not wholly right, but she was still sane enough to realise that the belief was based on nothing more than a desire that it should be so. The overwhelming feeling she had for him was certainly not based on a careful assessment of his character. She knew nothing about him that he had not conveyed to her himself. All the rest was conjecture. Now there was this story, odd and frightening as the doctor told it.

"I've startled you," said young Dr. Ledbury. "Perhaps I ought not to have put it quite so badly. But do look after her, Mademoiselle Robert. Don't forget I'm trusting her to your care absolutely. Don't trouble to see me downstairs. I can very well let myself out. Go in to her now, will you? She really is quite the most wonderful person."

The final remark escaped him involuntarily and Margot

smiled. So Zoff had made another conquest. All her life Margot had watched that happen. Young men, old men, men who had reached the middle age when women bored them, they all fell for Zoff and all in the same surprised and boyish way.

"I'll come tomorrow, tell her," said the doctor, disappearing down the stairs. "Tell her not to worry about anything, anything at all."

His voice faded and she heard his feet reach the tiles of the hall.

"Margot!" The thrilling whisper sped across the landing. "Isn't he *superbe*?"

It was Zoff, of course. She was standing on the threshold of her bedroom, swaddled in shawls, her black eyes shining out of foaming Shetland wool. Margot hurried over to her.

"You'll catch cold," she said. "What are you doing wandering about in your nightie?"

Zoff's strong fingers caught her arm and they went into the huge warm room together. Zoff was laughing.

"I wanted you to see him," she said. "When poor Cortot played Hernani to my Doña Sol, he had just such a profile, believe it or not. He was just such a man, too. The good God gave him beauty and said, 'My friend, that is enough, be content. Someone else must have the intelligence.'"

"But, darling, is it wise to have that kind of *doctor*?" Margot was inveigling her toward the mighty bed, with its dolphins, its cupids and rococo cornucopias. Zoff did not answer immediately but indicated a motif on the headboard of the edifice with some pride.

"Wet flowers growing out of a golden cream horn," she said devastatingly. "Kit would have married me when his wife died—I think of her in hell sometimes, do you know—if my taste had not been so horrible. I *adore* this bed! The poor, beautiful doctor is stupid, you say?"

"No, I didn't, as you very well know. I only felt that you might have had someone more experienced."

"I will when I have pain." Zoff climbed into her couch with considerable agility. "Just now I am only tired. When I have pain I will endure an old and ugly doctor whose brains stick out in lumps all over his head. Meanwhile, this boy is charming. He talks so much, do you notice? It never stops, the pleasant British voice. And he is so delighted to be attending me. I am his star patient. While he is killing others doubtless he tells them about me. There, now I am warm again. Sit here beside me on the bed, *petite*."

Margot settled herself obediently. The stiff folds of her gown made a dark shadow on the peach coverlet.

"What about these attacks, Zoff?"

Zoff's hand closed over her own, but the reply did not come immediately and when it did it was uncharacteristically evasive.

"They are both old women, Gen'vieve and the doctor. It is quite possible that I fainted only." She was sitting upright, her eyes thoughtful as she contemplated the shadows at the far end of the room.

"Do you expect me to believe that?"

"I do not care what you believe, *chérie*." Her hand was still firm and possessive. "I do not want to talk about the two contretemps. It is even possible that I am a little frightened." She shivered, a gesture so unlike herself as to be startling.

"Don't." The girl spoke sharply. "You'll frighten me. Would you like me to call Gen'vieve? Where is she?"

"Gone up to her own room. Don't call her. She's an old fool, Margot. No eyes, no nose, no ears. Nothing but a big heart. Poor Zoff, surrounded by fools! What else did my doctor tell you? Well?"

"He said you were not to see Denis any more."

"Ah. And do you think that is wise?"

"I?"

"Yes, you, mademoiselle. You, my *petite*." She was suddenly at her fiercest, her eyes black diamonds again. "Do you agree?"

"I don't know." Margot released herself gently. "If he upsets you, of course——"

"Upsets me!" Zoff mimicked her contemptuously.

"Well, at any rate, you're not going to see him. That's been arranged. We'll pack him off tonight if you like. I don't think he can realise it, you know. He——"

"Margot." A vigorous hand caught her wrist again. "I am disgustingly old, and the shame of being old is that one is still young. One still *knows*."

"Darling, once and for all, as far as Denis and I are concerned there is nothing to know."

"How true is that?"

"Utterly. I told you. Some months ago we had some greasy spaghetti together and talked of *la patrie*. We met twice."

"To meet once," said Zoff, "to see each other from the window of a taxicab, is enough for love if one is alive."

"Not nowadays, dearest." The girl dropped a kiss on the white shawl. "You're a romantic, Zoff. We don't love so extravagantly in these hard times."

"But how sordid!" Zoff was becoming herself again as she was half reassured. "It is a good thing," she went on more seriously. "All those D'Hivers were strange men. The grandfather of this Denis, my first husband. *Mon Dieu*, what a monster when once one knew! But be careful, Margot. There was always something in that family in the men—the women, my dear, were dull provincials and so *ugly*—which was extraordinary. They could hold spellbound any woman for a little time. They held in their faces, in their voices, in their thick, strong bodies a sort of promise—do you understand?—a promise of something unknown and fearful and yet so beautiful it broke one's heart."

She closed her eyes and the lids, which were like Victor's, showed paper-fine. Presently she laughed.

"I am *jeune fille* again, so undignified. *Jeune fille*, with great bags under the eyes and no hair to speak of. What a horrible sense of humour he has, the *bon Dieu*.

Well, as I was saying, the D'Hivers had a charm which was dangerous to the warm and impulsive hearts. But when one tore back the sheet, what did one see? Not a cloven hoof—*ma foi!* one could have forgiven that—but a whole chest and stomach of stone. They do not care, that family. They have nothing to care with. They go their own way, and if you are in it they tread on your neck. I know. They have no fear and they never love in return."

Margot was listening to her, fascinated. This was a Zoff she hardly knew, speaking with a sincerity she seldom displayed. It was impossible not to be impressed by it. Up here in the big overscented room it was easy for Margot to slide back into the sophisticated world of her childhood in which Denis had no place. Presently she began to feel liberated, as if the bondage of the last few months had disappeared. It was an odd experience, as embarrassing and unreasonable as her first violent attraction. Zoff was still talking.

"Gen'vieve tells me that you go back to London tomorrow for a luncheon. It is in your honour, I hope?"

"Yes, at the Ivy. Monsieur Bonnet wants to tell me I have been a clever girl."

"Naturally. What will you wear?"

They talked clothes for some time. Zoff was in tremendous form, racy, practical and inspired by turns, and gradually under her magic touch the exciting world of fashion and the theatre slid into focus again for Margot, and all its old appeal returned. The weariness of travel, the long hours, exacting parts, even the essential loneliness of the artist, disappeared before the glow and promise of the haze of glory at the top of the tree.

By the time Madame Zoffany was prepared to attempt to sleep all the alarms of the evening were in the background. Margot returned to them with something of dismay. She took up a tray from the bed table.

"I'll take this down for Gen'vieve," she said. "She's

growing old, Zoff, and the stairs are killing her. We must get someone younger to do the running about."

"Nonsense, she's younger than I. She is tired because she is so fat, the great elephant." The exacting Zoff, who was so mean over little things, had returned with a rush. "It does her good," she said airily. "Good night, *petite*. Come and kiss me in the morning so I may see your hat."

Margot left her lying peacefully in the outrageous bed and went down the staircase to the basement. Everywhere was so very well lit that a shocking suspicion occurred to her that poor Kit must be footing the power bill. There was no escaping it; Zoff was quite abominable in some matters.

She found the kitchen cluttered by a great charcoal stove which was obviously a recent acquisition. Another demand on Kit, no doubt. The room was deserted when she entered it, but at the sound of her step Felix appeared from a pantry. He looked startled and sulky, and to her amazement she saw his cheeks were wet. In the twenty years she had known him she had seen him in many conditions of emotional deshabille, but secret weeping was something new.

"Why, Felix, what's the matter?" she demanded. "What is it? What's happened?"

He stood before her, a forlorn figure in shirt sleeves. There were grease spots on his tie, on his waistcoat, even on the felt slippers on his sore feet. The moisture on his pallid face was both pathetic and ridiculous.

"I am low-spirited," he said, the French enhancing the statement. "It is nothing, nothing at all. Unless" —he hesitated hopefully—"perhaps Mademoiselle could influence Madame?"

"I could try, anyway," she said encouragingly. "Cheer up, Felix. What in the world is it?"

He perched himself on the kitchen table and brought long hands into play as he talked. Everything about him save his eyes, which were sombre, was slightly absurd.

"Mademoiselle Margot, it is like this. I have heard

from Grenoble that my old father is very shaky. The time must come soon when he will die."

"I am sorry, Felix. I didn't know."

"Oh well, he is old, mademoiselle. He has had a good life. The end comes to everybody."

She digested this philosophy and began to understand.

"He still has the bakery, has he?"

*"Précisément.* There is the little shop which you remember. I took you there when you were a small child. It has been done up recently and is doing a good trade. There is also the house where I was born. It is full of fine furniture of which my poor dead *maman* was inordinately proud. Behind that there is the orchard, with splendid apples, planted by my father. And behind that there is a magnificent piece of land. It is a property, you understand."

"Yes, I do, Felix, I do perfectly." Margot was entirely serious. She could remember the little white baker's shop with the scrubbed shelves and the great trays of apple pastry in the window. Squat and secure, it lay by the side of the busy road, a symbol of the smallness, and the smugness, and the security of petit bourgeois France. She put the pertinent question.

"Who is at home down there now?"

"Everybody." His agony was ludicrous. "My eldest brother is in the house with his wife and children; my second brother has moved into the town and is in lodgings near by, working at a factory; my sister who married the carpenter is at the end of the street; and my other sister's little farm is not more than twenty kilometres away in the country, and every Sunday she brings her family to see their grandfather. Mademoiselle, you will admit I should be there."

"Of course. The inheritance is assured by law, we know, but it is foolish not to be present as soon as any division is even considered. The mother bird brings the worm for all the mouths in the nest, but it goes hardly with the fledgling who is lying underneath the tree."

The simile was unfortunate. Felix looked very like a

fledgling in his bedraggled black waistcoat and blue shirt sleeves. Margot was sorry for him.

"Won't Madame let you go?" she enquired.

"But yes." He was voluble. "I may go tomorrow. But if so, I am not to return and Madame strikes out of her will the five hundred thousand francs which is bequeathed to me. It is much too much to lose, mademoiselle. But meanwhile my sister writes to say my father grows very weak."

It was a problem. Margot knew Zoff far too well to venture any rash promises.

"I'll try, Felix," she said. "I must go to London in the morning, but I'll talk to her as soon as I get back. Don't count on anything, but we'll do what we can. After all, Madame is a Frenchwoman. She understands these family matters."

"Yet it would not appear so from her manner toward Monsieur Denis." The muttered words were hardly audible and were clearly meant to be an aside, but Margot's face tingled as though she had received a little blow. This must be the explanation of Denis's visits, of course, but she was loth to accept it. The whole matter was suddenly very distasteful. Felix continued to look piteous.

"It is too much to lose," he repeated. "I have been with Madame so long. Yet I should only be away for a little time."

"I'll see," she repeated. "I'll try. I can't promise to succeed, but I will try."

He sighed as if he knew already what the result would be, and she came away, leaving him still sitting there on the table, sullen bitterness in his eyes.

## FOUR

The hall was bright and so silent when she came up into it that the sighing of her long skirts on the tiles sounded almost noisy. She was not at all happy. Things were bad in the house. Everyone was frustrated and a sense of unrest and vague menace was growing stronger all the time. She had given up thinking about Denis. Every time he came into her mind she thrust him out again. That folly had been scotched, she decided, fortunately in time before she had done anything silly. The escape from the petty cruelty which had tormented her was a great relief, but all the same it had left a very weary emptiness behind it.

She turned into the drawing room expecting to find them all there, still talking about the clock if she knew Victor. From her new mood of safety she was prepared to regard Denis dispassionately and was half looking forward to, half dreading, the experience. On the threshold she paused. A gust of rain-soaked air met her and she closed the door behind her quickly as the draught blew the silk window curtains out into the room.

She saw Denis at once. He was alone, standing before the French windows, which were wide open. His back was toward her and he was looking out into the wet darkness, but he turned at the sound of the latch and she saw a frown sweep over his forehead as he caught sight of her.

He came back into the room reluctantly.

"I hope you don't mind this. I don't think the rain's actually coming in." His deep, pleasant voice was unusually brusque and the ease which was one of his principal characteristics was strained.

"No, I don't mind." She moved over to the fire as she spoke and stood on the rug, her fair head framed against the prim carving of the mantelpiece. The room was chilly, and here too the brightness of the lights shed a hard unfriendliness over the mellow wood and faded colouring of chintz and tapestry.

He started to stroll toward her but hesitated and half turned, as if he were contemplating taking up his old position before the windows again.

"Where are the others?" she demanded and was irritated to find her voice husky.

"Soubise has driven Sir Kit down to the town. They're going to drag some poor wretched clockmaker away from his supper. Someone's torn up one of the family heirlooms."

He changed his mind again and wandered down toward her as he spoke. At that moment she was more vividly aware of the look of the man than ever before. One of Zoff's remarks leapt into her mind. "In their faces, in their voices, in their thick, strong bodies they held a sort of promise..."

She took a vigorous hold of herself and her smile was casual.

"It's a pity about the clock."

"Oh, you knew, did you?" His eyes met hers briefly. "Yes, I suppose it is. I hate that sort of baroque decoration, all gold piecrust. But I don't like the damage, either. It's a little mad, isn't it? It jolts one. However, this house is reeking with that sort of thing. That's why I opened the windows, I suppose."

"To let the baroquerie out?" she enquired, laughing. Her face was raised to his and the light fell on her skin and on her beautiful mouth and made narrow blue jewels of her eyes. She was unconscious of the effect and of the sudden colour which came into her face as his expression changed.

"No," he said, clinging to each trivial word as if it were some sort of life line. "No, I opened the window because for some reason tonight I could not breathe."

The final word choked him and he put out his hand helplessly.

The kiss was very gentle. His arms folded round her as she leaned toward him, and the first startled flicker of surprise in her eyes gave way to another emotion before her lids covered them.

For a minute he held her hard, hurting her, hugging her against him as if he were afraid she must vanish. And then suddenly he drew back roughly and turned away down the room.

"I'm sorry," he said.

Margot did not move. Everything that had once seemed to set her free from him, Zoff's tirade, the doctor's query, Felix's bland assumption, disappeared as if none of them had existed, and she felt again as she had done in her cabin coming home across the Atlantic, when every mile meant only a mile nearer to him.

"I love you, Denis."

"I know." He swung round to her furiously. "I saw, just now."

"And you don't love me, I suppose?"

"No."

She was not angry, not even hurt. The word glanced off her like a shaft of straw. She stood straight, unutterably happy, her lips parted, her eyes shining with laughter.

"That's—not true."

He came close to her, holding her again, looking down at her covetously, smiling a little, his square chin drawn down.

"Just now you saw too, I suppose."

She nodded and he kissed her again. He was shaking a little and she could feel their hearts beating.

"But it won't do," he said with sudden weariness. "It won't do, Margot. There's too much against it. You're all tied up to Victor, for one thing, aren't you?"

"No. Not now. Not since yesterday."

He looked at her sharply and she could see the question in his eyes and feel him trying not to ask it. Her generosity was boundless. Her love was so great it engulfed all the small reluctances. She answered the query before he put it.

"I think it must have been because of you, Denis. I wasn't admitting it at the time. Did you come here because of me?"

"No!" he said so violently that she knew he was lying. "No, certainly not. I don't want to love you, Margot."

"But you do, Denis?"

He found her hands and bent his head over them.

"Oh, darling," he said, "ever since I saw you . . . and so hopelessly, do you know."

135

Voices in the hall outside cut in on them brutally. He stepped back but did not release her hands.

"We've got to talk," he murmured urgently. "When? They say you're going to London early."

"I'll be home in the afternoon," she whispered back. "You'll be here?"

A door slammed and the curtains shuddered. She released herself from him gently and felt an absurd but poignant sense of loss as her hands were freed.

"Yes." His eyes were still on her face, still helplessly vulnerable, but there was a shadow in them. "Yes, I'll be here."

Sir Kit opened the door.

"The clock is on this wall, if you'll come in," he was saying to someone behind him. "I do most earnestly hope you'll be able to do something. Come along, come along. Good heavens, what a draught! Is that you, Victor? Come in, my boy, for goodness' sake, and shut those doors behind you."

As the two on the hearthrug turned slowly round, Victor Soubise stepped in through the French doors and began to close and fasten them. He glanced over his shoulder at Margot as he shot the upper bolt, his face impassive.

"I came in this way after putting up the car," he said briefly. "It's nearer." His voice was flat and unrevealing. There was no telling if the observation was an apology, a reproach, or simply a statement of fact.

## FIVE

Hercule Bonnet, manager of the Beaux Arts company, brought Margot down after the lunch in the chauffeur-driven hired Daimler he always used when in London. He was in the top of his form and there had been no getting away from him. At the end of the party he had pushed his eyeglass into one of the deep sockets—they always look painted they were so dark—and had given

her a flash of white teeth as he announced his intention
of coming down to Bridgewyck to pay his respects to
the "*chère maîtresse.*"

On the way down he had talked all the time, his
plump hands dipping and swooping like sea gulls over
the dome of his grey waistcoat as he told her what he
was going to say to Zoff.

He was overdressed, as was usual in England, since,
so he said, he believed the natives expected it of a
Frenchman.

"I have the exquisite courtesy," he would explain half
seriously. "That is why I am beloved wherever I go."

Margot was his discovery of the moment. She was his
little pigeon, his cabbage, his queen. He was about, he
insisted, to fling himself at Zoff's feet to thank her for
bequeathing her genius on such a pupil. He was a trifle
drunk, of course, but only to the point of elation.
Margot had nothing to do but to look as if she were
listening, and so far, for the best part of the journey, she
had not missed a cue.

She was so happy she almost told him the reason, but
he gave her no opportunity to make that mistake. His
theme was the future and his voice never ceased.

As the car nosed its way through the endless little
townships which had become the suburbs of the city,
she lay back in the cushions, one ear on his chatter and
all the rest of her conscious self obsessed with delight.
It was madness to be in love like this, she reflected, her
eyes dancing; in love as if one were sixteen, as if no one
else mattered, as if every one of these dazzling successes
which Bonnet was so cheerfully prophesying was well
lost for an hour with Denis. It was lunacy, of course,
delirious nonsense, proverbially ephemeral, and yet it
was so very sweet.

And behind the ecstasy was something real and inescapable and forever. She was sure of it. It had made a
little blanket over her heat. She could still hear Denis's
voice behind the florid periods which Bonnet was intoning
at her side.

"The English drowned the French." The deep voice sounded through the thin one: "...*ever since I saw you*...*and so hopelessly*..."

The words shocked her still. Even in memory they disturbed her breathing. They were precious and wholly ridiculous, for nothing was hopeless now. Bonnet's chatter cut into her day-dreaming as the car turned into the familiar road and she sat up.

"'*Chère doyenne des arts suprême*,' I shall whisper," he was rehearsing happily. "'*Maîtresse de milles coeurs*...' Eh, we arrive, do we? Is this the house?"

Margot spoke to the chauffeur, who turned into the drive and brought the big car to a standstill before the porch.

"Permit me." Bonnet was in gallant mood. All vehicles presented certain embarrassments to his plumpness, but he was determined to hand her out himself, so there was some delay as he was first extricated and set panting on the step.

Margot let him assist her and they were standing together in the conservatory when the front door was thrown open.

Felix stood before them, gibbering. He was only just recognisable. There was no colour in his face at all and his eyes were blank. He stared at Bonnet and turned wildly to Margot.

"That is not *monsieur le docteur*," he said stupidly. "Mademoiselle, where is the doctor?"

Her pulse missed a stroke and a chill crept over her.

"What is it, Felix?" She heard her own voice speaking very quietly. "Quickly, what is it? Is Zoff ill?"

"Mademoiselle, she is dead." He was dragging her into the hall with the feeble, plucking hands of a frightened old man.

"Oh no, *no*," she said, as if somehow the word would make it true. At her side she was just aware of Bonnet's scandalised face wearing a ludicrous expression of disappointment. "Where is Sir Kit?"

"Mademoiselle, he has not been here since before

138

*déjeuner.*" Felix was shaking visibly and appeared to be about to collapse. "There is no one here but me and Gen'vieve. It was Gen'vieve who first found Madame and she who telephoned *monsieur le docteur*. I am waiting for him, but it is of no use. Madame is dead. I have seen her."

"Where is Denis?"

"Mademoiselle, Monsieur Denis is gone."

Unless she dreamed it, the words were shouted.

"It was after he left Madame's room that we found her suffocated. There was a pad over her face and her hands were folded. It was then, after Monsieur Denis had gone out of this door with Madame's case in his hands, that we found her."

"With Madame's case?" she echoed blankly.

"But yes, Margot." He had given up civilities, and the use of her name reminded her that he had known her from babyhood. "Her green case, the bag. The leather case with the drawer underneath."

She stared at him, her brows drawn down into a line.

"Where the jewels were?"

"Where the jewels were."

In the bewildered silence a step sounded on the stone behind them and she swung round to confront the young doctor. He was breathless and his eyes were furious.

"So you let it happen," he said bitterly, peering contemptuously into her face. "You were warned and it was under your nose, and yet you let it happen."

Margot remained staring at him. Her cheeks were transparently white and her eyes looked enormous under the pale feather fringe of her Lelong model. She felt as if a page were turning back in the course of her life. It was as though a digression had ended suddenly, hurling her once more into the main story.

"But I told you," the doctor was saying. "I gave you the most explicit instructions. I said the patient was not to be allowed to see that man." He bent over her as he spoke. With bright patches of colour on his cheek-bones, he looked like an infuriated archangel.

She continued to meet his gaze helplessly. She was vividly aware of negligence but of absurdity also.

"You're making a dreadful mistake," she said. "Denis can't have had anything to *do* with it. Of course he didn't. You don't understand."

He drew back from her.

"This is hardly the moment for discussion, don't you think, or do you?" The pomposity displayed his antago-nism like a weapon and he brushed past her and strode on to the foot of the stairs. With one hand on the banister, he turned and looked back. "Have the police been sent for yet?" he asked Felix.

"No, *monsieur le docteur*. Gen'vieve telephoned for you, that was all."

"I see. Will you come up, please?" He stood aside for the old man and mounted the stairs behind him. Margot watched them go.

It was some moments before she remembered Bon-net. A cough at her side startled her and she turned to find him looking at her, a mixture of chagrin and honest alarm on his plump face. He had no need to explain. She understood immediately and went to his rescue.

"Go back," she said. "After all, you've hardly been in the house. I shall simply say a friend brought me to the door."

He was grateful but still very embarrassed.

"*Chérie*, I wish I could stay. What a tragedy! What a disaster! She had quarrelled with someone, *n'est-ce pas?*"

"No," she said quickly. "No, it's a mistake of the doctor's."

"I see. I think, though, he intends to call in the *flics*, that one."

"He does, doesn't he?" she agreed absently, her mind not so much on that alarming possibility as on the awful fact of Zoff's passing. "You get away, Hercule. There is no reason for you to be mixed up in this, none in the world."

"Perhaps it would be as well." He was loth to relinquish his role of gallant, but prudence advised him strongly. No one understood more about the benefits and the dangers of publicity.

Seeing him standing there hesitating focused somehow the whole situation for Margot. She was aware of every detail. The ornate hall, transversed with huge modern patterns in sunlight from the open door into the conservatory, was vivid for an instant. She knew what the scene must be like upstairs too, where the old servants and the doctor must be standing round the bed.

Bonnet took her hand and held it tightly. Behind the mass of affectations and shrewdnesses which made up most of the man, there appeared for an instant a fleeting warm reality.

"Ring me up if there's anything I can do," he said, his sincerity underlining the danger.

"I shall hold you to that, Hercule," she said.

He nodded. "You may, my dear. But now I shall go." He raised her hand briefly to his lips and trotted out to the car. She heard the door slam a moment later and then the whirr of the starter. For a second she hesitated, and then, laying her bag and gloves on a side table, went quietly up the stairs.

Zoff lay stiffly on her golden bed. The peach-coloured coverlet was drawn up to her waist and a blue brocaded dressing jacket was wrapped softly about her breast and shoulders. Her hands were folded. Her face was calm, and, as it had never been in life, oddly gentle apart from a certain accentuation of her big features, the nose knife-sharp and the cheekbones prominent. It was difficult not to think her asleep.

She was not quite smiling but her wide mouth was soft and secretive.

At the end of the bed Margot stood with Genevieve and marvelled at her dignity. Death had shown none of its derisive cruelty here. There was no pathos, no absurdity; only majesty and peace and resignation. It was even difficult to think of weeping. This was something to admire.

The extraordinariness of the fact did not strike the girl. She was stunned by the shock of her loss and stood quiet, her arm round Genevieve's shoulders, holding her hard brown hand.

From the bed, the stones in the dead woman's rings winked and trembled, startlingly alive against the quiet flesh.

The doctor was moving about at the other end of the room. He and Felix had thrown open the windows and the curtains were swinging out in the stiff breeze, filling the room with movement. At the moment the two men were at the armoire and were bending down before the empty shelf where Zoff had kept her battered green dressing case. She had always insisted on having it there regardless of any valuables it contained, and relying on the "secret" drawer, a device which would not have deceived a squirrel, let alone a child.

Felix was whispering, explaining the details to the younger man. Margot and Genevieve were only just aware of them. They stood close together, quite still, looking at the bed. As with most great personalities, Zoff had seemed immortal to her intimates, and since in death her personality had vanished, only a stranger had been left behind. The phenomenon had stupefied them. They could not credit it, could not believe the one irrevocable fact, Zoff was gone. They both felt that at any moment she must sit up and laugh at their terror, flinging back her head to show the gold-crowned tooth at the back of her mouth as she delighted in the outrageous joke.

It was Genevieve who broke the spell.

"She was just so when I found her," she whispered. "Like this, as if she was in a play. I took the towel off her face and saw her. God forgive me, I couldn't touch her after that. I put it back."

"But it's so incredible." The doctor's voice, loud, young and impatient, startled them. He had been waiting for Genevieve to recover herself and now seized on the first sign. "I don't understand it," he said, coming round in front of them. "Do you mean to tell me you smelled nothing at all? Why, even now the room reeks of it. The towel must have been saturated."

Margot trembled. She had been vaguely aware of something odd in the house ever since she reached the stairhead, and now at last it took a definite shape in her mind. Once one faced it, it was inescapable. Everywhere, clinging to the draperies, eddying in the draught, fighting and conquering the hundred perfumes with which Zoff's belongings were always drenched, was the sweet, horrible stench of the operating theatre.

"Ether," she said huskily.

The doctor raised his eyes to hers. "No. Just old-fashioned chloroform, I think. Can't you smell it, Gen'vieve?"

"No. I smell nothing."

"Gen'vieve has no sense of smell," put in Felix, who had joined the group. "Not for many years now."

The doctor caught his breath and glanced again at Margot.

"Is that true?"

"I don't know. I suppose so. We used to tease her and say so. Zoff—Zoff said so."

"But, good heavens, don't you see what this means?" In his excitement his pomposity dropped from him like a false moustache, she reflected bitterly. He was thrilled to find himself a detective. "Don't you see, it must have happened before? This must be the explanation of the other two attacks. I didn't notice it then because each time Gen'vieve had got her propped up by an open window and the place aired, as far as it can be with all this scent about, before I arrived. On this occasion the fellow used so much of the stuff that he succeeded in killing her very quickly and I got here before the fumes were dispersed."

143

Margot turned on him. "Oh, you can't say things like that," she said breathlessly. "You can't make wild accusations. You've no possible way of knowing if it's true."

"My good girl"—the hostility swept back into his eyes—"it's rather obvious, isn't it? Zoff told us herself that he had made two attempts to kill her, and like fools we didn't believe her. Now he has succeeded. He's probably a lunatic," he went on gravely. "He may have tried to be subtle to begin with, but in the end he became so reckless he drenched her with the stuff. Who else could have done it? Chloroform doesn't lie about in ordinary houses. Yet it would be the simplest thing in the world for him to get hold of, and would have been very difficult to trace after a short period."

He silenced Genevieve, who was about to speak, and went smoothly on, still speaking to Margot.

"You don't want the scandal, of course (I don't blame you), nor do I. But neither of us can help it. This is murder. He even took some jewellery, I understand."

The girl did not speak. She was battling with an extraordinary conviction that something inevitable was taking place. It was not that she believed the story for an instant, but she realised that it was an explanation which must occur to most people, and somewhere she had the impression that it had all had to happen like this.

The doctor left her and returned to Felix, who was busy at a small wall safe at the far end of the room. He had opened it and was examining the plush and leather cases within.

"We must get on to the police at once." The doctor still spoke with that suppressed excitement which jarred upon them all. "They'll pick him up on an air station, I expect. Work out a rough inventory of the things that are missing, Felix. They'll need that."

Margot glanced at the bed again and came to a sudden decision. It had occurred to her that probably she was the only living person in the household who knew where Denis lived. The police would find him through the hospital, but it was quite possible that neither Genevieve nor Felix would remember even that in their present state. At any rate, it would take a little time to find him. Even she did not know the address, but he had once pointed out the house he shared with a dozen other students and she thought she could find it again. If she went at once, the probability was that she would catch him first. One thing, at least, was obvious. He must come back at once to clear himself before any more of this crazy circumstantial evidence piled up against him. She had no idea why he had left the house or where he had gone, but if there was a chance of finding him, she felt it worth taking.

She glanced at the doctor. He was still absorbed in Felix's discovery. Genevieve had crept up to the bed head again, a silk shawl in her hands. For the moment Margot was unnoticed. Without looking back, she walked quietly out of the room.

Her grey-clad figure passed down the stairs as silently as a ghost. Her feet made no sound on the tiles of the hall and the street door closed gently behind her.

Bridgewyck central police station was a yellow brick building at the end of the main street, next door to the Regal Cinema and opposite the subway to the electric railway. By one of those pieces of pure chance which figure so often in official police reports, as if Fate herself were on the side of the authorities, Inspector Lee was standing looking idly out of his window on the first floor when his telephone bell rang. He could reach the instrument from where he stood and was still on his feet, his glance fixed absently on the opposite pavement, when the sergeant downstairs put through the call from Clough House.

While the doctor was still talking, his voice brittle with an affectation of curt authority, Inspector Lee's long-sighted eyes alighted on Margot Robert. She was hurrying down the pavement, her slender body thrown forward by her high heels, her hands grasping her big grey bag. As he watched her she turned into the dark mouth of the subway and disappeared. Lee recognised her and remembered the one thing about her which had interested him. She was the girl who had made the old woman change her mind about charging her grandson. He prided himself on his hunches and he swung round, holding the phone to his breast.

"Carpenter," he said, "quickly! A girl's just gone down to the tube station. Grey costume, grey feathered hat, pretty, West End actress type, fair, five foot two, about twenty years old. After her. Follow all the way. Ring me back. You may just do it."

A shadow in the back of the room slid out from behind a desk, reached for the hat which lay upon it, and passed out of the door obediently. While the telephone still crackled at him the inspector noted his man cross the road and enter the station. He glanced at the clock over the door. Two and a half minutes. The trains ran every eight. The odds were on Carpenter making it, he decided.

He returned to the telephone. "All right. Thank you, Doctor. I'll be with you in six or seven minutes. Keep everything as it is, of course. Let no one in or out. What? Oh, clear case, is it? Well, that saves us a lot of trouble, doesn't it? But we can't be too careful. Just see all doors are locked. Is Miss Robert there? What? She's downstairs, is she? She's——what? Oh. I see, very upset. Very well, sir. Thank you. Good-bye."

## SIX

Dower Street looked as if it had been drawn in blue chalks when Margot turned into it. She hurried, unaware of the quiet man in the crumpled suit who trudged behind her, keeping pace easily with her shorter steps. The deep blue of the northern twilight spread everywhere. Even the grey houses and the gleaming, tire-polished roads had taken on the steely colour of the sky. Street lamps were as yet little lemon patches in the amethyst. They stretched on into the distance like a necklace of yellow beads.

Detective Officer Carpenter saw the phone box and noted it as he had noted every other they had passed since they left the Underground and he had all but lost the girl in the crowds. She was looking up at the houses now. This was more promising. She was not seeking a number, though, but was peering at each façade as if she hoped to recognize it. Once she hesitated and he was puzzled. But no, she had changed her mind and was off again, himself at a safe distance behind her.

Ah, now she had found it. He could see the relief in the sag of her shoulders as she turned to climb up the three worn steps to the door. He paused to light a cigarette and kept his eyes on her.

Margot stood hesitating on the stone platform. The door stood wide open and she was confronted by the misty cavern of what had once been a fine vestibule. There was only one bell push, a single button in a tarnished saucer of brass. She pressed it doubtfully and far away in the basement a bell rang hollowly, but there was no other result whatever. She was about to try again when there was a patter of footsteps in front of her at the far end of the passage as someone raced down a stairway toward her. She stepped back to save herself.

"I say, I'm sorry." The voice was very young and she found herself looking into an inquisitive face under untidy hair. He was barely twenty and ostentatiously dishevelled. "D'you really want to come in here?" he enquired with the laborious roguishness of his age. "Are you sure?"

"Well, I want to see Mr. Cotton, if I may."

"Oh." He was deflated. "Oh well, I'll see to that for you. You stand here while I get the light on." His voice ran on pleasantly as he moved, and presently a grimy light bulb leapt into life and she saw a well-worn strip of lino between drab walls leading to a staircase beyond. "Please come in here."

Her guide had become more formal now that he could see her.

"This is the only reception room in the house, I'm afraid. We use it to interview guardians and taxgatherers. Don't let it lean on you. It's our landlord's décor, not ours."

He held a door open for her and chattered on without permitting her to speak.

"I'll get Cotton," he said. "Sit down, if the chairs aren't too dusty. Shan't be a moment."

He raced off like a puppy and she heard him shouting for Denis from the foot of the staircase. Margot stood waiting, her hand on the mahogany table which filled most of the ill-lit room. The rest of the furnishings were lost on her. She was listening, her head down. Not once did it occur to her that he might not be here. She waited confidently for his step and the sound of his voice. Ever since the first shock of the tragedy she had been living in a half-world in which only very simple things were ordinary and in which the great events surrounding her swept her along with them without help. Now for a second all the dreadful lunacy of the situation confronted her intelligence. It was as though she had been climbing a precipice and had suddenly looked down. She grasped the full danger, the full significance, of everything she had learnt since leaving Bonnet's Daimler. All the nerves in her face tingled as if a cold wind had touched her.

Just then, outside in the street, Detective Officer Carpenter decided that the time had arrived when it was safe to telephone. Meanwhile, in the passage, the obliging student shouted again. This time he was rewarded. A door opened on one of the upper floors and light footsteps echoed on the linoleum-covered stairs. There were a few muttered words and then the door swung in on her. She turned to meet him.

She had no idea of the unexpected picture she made, her elegance shaming the dingy room but her face white and strained under the frivolous hat. She put out her hands to him.

"Thank God you're here," she said incoherently. "Quickly, Denis, we've got to hurry."

The final word faded on her lips. He did not take her hands but turned to close the door behind him before standing back against it. He was as pale as she was. His ugly chin was thrust out and his eyes were darker than she had ever seen them. Their expression was quite new to her.

"I didn't expect you," he said with appalling distinctness. "I'm sorry you came."

For a little while she said nothing, but stood quiet, catching her emotions together and holding them like streamers in the wind.

"You'll have to come back," she said at last, as soon as she was sure of her voice. "The sooner the better."

"I'm afraid that's quite impossible."

The light straggling out from under the solid old-fashioned shade over the table, caught on the bunched muscles on the corners of his jaw. But for that, his tone might have sounded impersonal.

"But the police——" she began and was cut short by his laugh.

"Darling," he said, "need we have the melodrama?"

She almost laughed herself with the relief. She had not known before how real her unadmitted fear had been.

"You don't know?" she said, unable to prevent her voice from rising a little. "Of course, you don't know. Zoff is dead, Denis."

She saw his eyes widen and then the veils of reserve crept over them, blotting out all expression.

"Dead?" he echoed softly, and she felt him become very wary. After a long pause he said quietly: "No, I didn't know."

He was looking at the wall behind her head and there was a new stolidity about him. In the midst of her bewilderment it came into her mind that he was by no means inexperienced where suspicion was concerned. There had been the *Citation à l'ordre de l'armée*, his "mention in despatches." She remembered the extract. *"Twice questioned by the Gestapo but disclosed nothing of value to the enemy."* He must have looked then much as he did now. The unfairness and incongruity of the comparison edged under her control.

"Don't you see that you've got to come at once?" she demanded, catching his sleeve. "I left just as the doctor was sending for the police. She didn't—die ordinarily, Denis. I came to find you before they did."

He stood looking down at her. His hands were in his pockets and she felt the unyielding iron of his arm under the sleeve in her fingers.

"She was very much alive when I left her," he said. "I'm sorry she's dead. She infuriated me, but I liked her. She was a great character."

The past tense hit the girl.

"I loved her," she said, and, without realising what was happening, began to cry. The tears flooded into her eyes and spilled over down her cheeks.

"Don't do that, for God's sake."

"No. No, I won't," she said ridiculously and felt blindly in her bag for a handkerchief. He pulled one out of his breast pocket and flicked it over to her.

"Now look here," he began as she struggled with herself, "do I understand that because of all the nonsense Zoff has been talking I am liable to be arrested? Is that what you're trying to tell me?"

"Yes."

"Very well. What am I expected to do in this benighted country? Walk up to the first bobby on the beat and give myself up?"

"No, of course not. You're expected to—well, to be in the house, to answer questions. To behave, in fact, as if you——"

"Were innocent. Is that what you're trying to say? Do you suspect me?"

"If I did," she said, "should I be here? Oh, Denis, what's the matter with you?"

The sudden direct appeal crept under his guard. His face twisted helplessly and he blundered toward her.

At that most unlucky of all moments Detective Officer Carpenter softly opened the door. He had an insignificant face, with bloodless lips and wet-looking eyes, and it appeared round the doorway as they sprang apart. After the first quick glance round he came in almost confidentially, shutting the door behind him.

"Mr. Denis Cotton?" he enquired in a much stronger voice than one might have expected to come out of such a shadow of a man.

Denis nodded and he turned to the girl.

"Mademoiselle Margot Robert."

"Ro-bert," she corrected him absently. Her eyes, frightened and comprehending, did not leave his face.

"Thank you," he said. "You'll have to excuse me, I'm afraid. I'm a detective officer of the Bridgewyck borough constabulary."

"Can I see your warrant?" Denis spoke too quickly. The pale eyebrows rose high and disapproving.

"I have no warrant. I'm not arresting anybody, sir." Save for the strong, harsh voice, he might have been a reproachful upper servant. "You can see my card, of course, if you want to. We've always got to be ready to show that when we're in plain clothes." He produced his credentials and Denis examined them.

"Well, what do you want?" he said briefly, handing them back.

Carpenter hesitated. His eyes were momentarily shifty, and the fantastic notion that he might be physically afraid of them was forced upon them both. There was a chaplet of sweat beads on his forehead.

"I have to ask you both to stay here," he said. "The inspector is on his way, and when he arrives you'll be asked to make statements in connection with a death which took place at Clough House, Hertford Street, Bridgewyck, this afternoon. You'll understand that I'm not cautioning you, but I must remind you that it will be my duty to make a note of anything you may say to one another in front of me."

He reeled off the official warning and shut his pale mouth tightly.

Denis looked at Margot. Most of his life had been spent in France, and this unexpected introduction to a new police procedure, with all its apparently meaningless formality, was bewildering.

"What's to prevent us walking out?" he enquired.

The plain-clothes man's shining eyes flickered at him.

"Nothing, sir, except that every police constable in the land would be looking for you in twenty minutes. Men on beats round here a good deal sooner," he said and passed his tongue over dry lips. "I should stay where you are, sir. It's only a question of making a statement. Perhaps you'd sit down, and the lady too. I'll keep standing just here if you don't mind."

He settled himself with his back against the door and they took chairs in silence. The dreary light from under the red shade made heavy shadows on their young faces. Margot kept quiet as long as she could, but at last words escaped her.

"Of course we're willing to make statements," she said, her clear voice pretty with its faint trace of accent. "Naturally we both want to help all we can. Mr. Cotton knew nothing about it until I told——"

"I shouldn't, miss—I beg your pardon, mademoiselle." The strident voice was not unkind. "Just wait for the inspector. He won't be long."

"But I have nothing to hide."

"I don't suppose you have, miss, but I rather expect he'll want to speak to you separately, if I make myself clear."

He did, of course. The unnatural quiet continued for a long time.

At last, when they were all three stiff from holding the same position, Denis stirred.

"We can smoke, I suppose?" he remarked.

The plain-clothes man jerked his head up.

"I can't stop you, sir, but I'd rather you didn't. Unless you'll have one of mine?" He offered a battered packet, and Margot watched Denis take one and accept a light. The veils were down over his eyes again and his mouth was expressionless.

The slam of a car door just outside in the street made her jump. The sound of heavy feet, first on the steps and then in the corridor, decided Carpenter. He opened the door with relief.

Lee came in with a sergeant behind him, and between them they filled the doorway with beef and authority. The inspector's square face was unsmiling, but there was distinct satisfaction in his expression as he took in the group. He was a worshipper of efficiency and today he appeared to have surpassed himself.

To Margot he came as a shock. She had not expected to find the same man in charge, and his few words to her in the corridor at Clough House returned to her as vividly as if a record had been played back to her: "You're the young lady who made Madame Zoffany change her mind, are you?" So he was prepared. The full story was already clear in his mind. Now, after finding her and Denis together like this, what on earth could he help thinking? She put her hand up to her mouth to smother the startled sound which she felt must come from it. No danger had ever been quite so vivid to her before. It was like the teetering moment of a car crash, just before the impact.

Inspector Lee cleared his throat. He was prepared to be courteous because he was making no arrest until he had the man safely in his own office and his own chief constable's sanction and approval. After the formal name-taking he issued the invitation which the law prescribes.

"I must ask you both to accompany me to Bridgewyck police station, where you will each be asked to make a statement. You know why, I think."

They nodded and he grunted his approval. It was growing very cold in the room despite the overcrowding.

The night air poured in from the open street door, bringing with it exhaust fumes and the purr of a running engine.

Denis caught Margot's eye and signalled to her to move, but he did not touch her hand or pick up her bag for her.

"Just one other thing before we go, Mr. Cotton." Lee's attempts to sound casual were more successful than his subordinate's. "When you left Clough House, Bridgewyck, this afternoon, you are reported as having carried a green leather bag. Is that correct?"

Margot caught her breath. All through her journey to town, and now while they had been waiting in silence, she had been trying to put that bag out of her mind.

There was a long pause, a little too long. Denis was hesitating. His face was white and his mouth almost ugly. At last he pulled a wallet out of his coat and took something from it. As they watched him he laid a slip of pink paper on the table. Lee took it up and looked at it. His heavy eyebrows rose.

"Charing Cross Station parcels office," he said softly. "Any explanation, Mr. Cotton?"

"Yes." Denis still sounded too cautious. "Madame Zoffany put the bag in my hands just as I was leaving her this afternoon at about a quarter past two. I didn't discover everything it contained until I was in a railway carriage coming to London. Because—because of what I found in it, I thought it would be safer in a parcels office than in my room here. It was too late to go to a bank, and you can see for yourself that this house is not very private. The street door is left open most of the day."

It was not a very convincing story. Even to Margot it sounded lame.

"I understand." Lee's satisfaction was becoming grim. "You are saying that this is the receipt for the green bag. Well, we'll go and fetch it, if you don't mind. Meanwhile, if you've no objection, I should like to send someone over your room here. Is this your only address?"

"In London, yes." Denis put a key on the table, and at a sign from Lee, Carpenter picked it up.

"Which door?" It was significant that he had dropped the "sir."

"Second floor, first on the left."

Carpenter went off upstairs and the inspector turned back to the two of them.

"If you're ready, we'll go," he said briefly.

It was not quite an arrest, yet Denis travelled down to Bridgewyck on the back seat of a police car, with a plain-clothes man on either side of him. Opposite, with his back to the driver, sat Lee, and next to him, overshadowed by his huge bulk, was Margot.

Outside Charing Cross the man next to the driver slipped out, to return in a minute or two with Zoff's shabby green jewel case. He handed it in to the inspector, who balanced it lovingly upon his knees for the rest of the journey. There was no talking.

## SEVEN

The waiting room at Bridgewyck police station was unpleasantly like a cell. A solid wooden seat ran round three sides of a small high-ceilinged chamber devoid of any sort of decoration. Not even a "Wanted" notice broke the monotony of the shabby green distemper.

Seated with his back to the fourth wall, a uniformed police sergeant worked at a small deal table, his bald head gleaming in the light from a naked bulb not far above it. He was writing steadily. In the last hour he had not once looked up.

Margot sat directly opposite him. She was still very pale, but her back was straight and there was a courageous gayety in the tilt of her feathered hat. The room might have been underground. No sound from the outside world penetrated the silence. It was now two hours by her watch since Denis had been taken upstairs to Lee's office, and during that time she had been quite alone.

In the beginning she had tried to review the situation coldly, arranging the facts as she knew them and attempting to piece together from them that other explanation which she prayed must be there. So far it had not emerged. The longer she considered, the more wretchedly simple the story remained. Zoff's old green jewel case was inescapable. Wherever she looked for help, there it was, inexplicable or damning.

As the minutes dragged on she gave up reasoning and let the dull misery of waiting engulf her. She dared not think about Zoff. That loss was too violent, too staggering, to be comprehended just yet.

The summons came at last. The bell on the table tinkled and the sergeant laid down his pen.

"Inspector Lee will see you now, miss. Will you follow me, please?"

The deceptive courtesy of policemen no longer bewildered her. She rose stiffly and they went out into a disinfectant-reeking corridor. She had decided upon her own part in the coming interview. The straight truth and the whole of it was the only possible line. It was not going to be easy. She realised that she would have to explain about herself and Denis, and that was a relationship so new that it was still very fragile and very precious. But after all, it was the vital factor in her own behaviour after Zoff's death, and to hide it would be to create mystery where there was none. She was dreading Lee on the subject. He was not the type to display much old-world delicacy, and she went in to meet him expecting the worst.

He was alone in a big airy room, seated behind his desk looking solid and forbidding, but he rose as she appeared and came toward her.

"Ah yes," he said with an unexpected lack of briskness, "Mademoiselle Robert. Sit down, won't you? My stenographer's gone down to the main office for a moment, but he won't be long. Have a cigarette?"

It was almost as if he had hoped not to see her at all. She looked at him blankly.

"No, no, thank you," she said. "You want me to make a statement?"

"If you will, as soon as my chap comes back to take it down. Just a short account of the facts as you know them. Nothing elaborate."

His attitude was surprising. He was making her feel as if she were wasting his time.

"I haven't much to tell."

"No. I don't suppose you have." He settled himself at the desk again and regarded her gloomily. "What time did you get back from your luncheon in London this afternoon?"

"I don't know exactly. Let me see, we lunched early—the French do, you know—oh, about three, I suppose."

"Three-five," he agreed, glancing at a sheet of paper on the desk. "The doctor arrived soon after, did he?"

"At the same time. We met on the step."

He nodded again, his eyes still on his notes.

"And then you decided to rush off again to town to tell Mr. Cotton all about it, is that right?" he said.

"Yes," she said and waited.

To her amazement, he seemed prepared to leave the matter there. He sat looking at her woodenly, as if no further remark occurred to him, and after a while his glance wandered to the door but no stenographer appeared.

"Have you arrested Denis?" The words were out of her mouth before she could stop them. His glance returned to her, the sheet of paper poised delicately in his thick fingers. For the first time he permitted a flicker of interest to appear in his round eyes.

"That's a funny thing for you to say, Mademoiselle Robert. Why do *you* say that?"

She found the slight emphasis which he laid on the word disconcerting.

"Is it true?"

He was frowning. "Did you expect it?" Suddenly he succeeded and she was exasperated.

"Well, the doctor was accusing him openly, which was why I went to fetch him. And then you rushed up after us and brought us back here in a car bristling with police, so I took it for granted you were going to make some such mistake," she said with asperity.

Something like revelation passed over the man's unexpectedly expressive face.

"I see," he said. "I see. You went to fetch him because you thought the doctor was accusing him. Not because you thought *he might be running away from you*."

Margot did not move. She heard the words and did not credit them. Lee, watching her closely, saw no reaction.

"No," she said and laughed a little. "That did not enter my mind."

He leant over the desk.

"Perhaps I've been making a mistake," he said with deceptive humility. "It's always rather difficult to get the picture, you know. I've not seen much of the personalities on this case yet, except, of course, Mr. Cotton's." He paused long enough to let the inference become clear and then went on, still with the same quiet affability.

"Let me see, you've only seen Mr. Cotton on three occasions since your childhood. And on the third, last night, in fact, you suddenly admitted a violent infatuation for him. That's so, isn't it?"

There was a moment of complete silence. Margot felt the blood rushing into her face as the savage stab at her vanity made its wound, but something horribly intelligent in the bright blue eyes warned her and she caught a glimpse of his purpose. She made an effort.

"I am a Frenchwoman, Inspector," she said. "We are supposed to be very temperamental. Sometimes, perhaps our infatuations do not last very long or go very deep."

158

Lee was disappointed. He almost showed it. His methods, which were well known and not altogether approved by his colleagues, were simple. In moments of deadlock it was his custom to stir up emotional trouble in every direction which presented itself, and then to wait for something to break. He was seldom entirely unsuccessful, but this time the results were not promising. Grudgingly he retraced his steps.

"You say you followed Cotton because the doctor accused him. What was the fact which made you think that accusation so dangerous?"

"His not being there," she said simply. "I thought he could at least be present to defend himself, for all our sakes."

Lee could have smacked her for her poise. He did the next best thing.

"Oh, I see, you were thinking of the scandal," he said easily. "You weren't worrying about the crime. You weren't thinking of this helpless old woman, who seems to have treated you like a daughter all your life."

It was too crude. He saw it himself and regretted it. Her expression did not alter. She sat there looking like a china ornament but revealing considerably more brain and stamina than most women possessed in his experience.

"I was not sure that there was a crime," she said.

"Eh? I don't get that." His careful gentleness was disappearing. "You don't think it was an accident, do you?"

"No, I suppose it couldn't have been."

"Or suicide?"

No, that was the one certainty. She shook her head. Zoff and suicide were incompatible. She had gloried in life too deeply ever to relinquish it voluntarily.

"Someone killed her," Lee said conversationally. "Someone you know. Someone in the house."

To his irritation, she did not dispute it. She had had some hours to think out that point. Strangers do not walk into crowded houses, chloroform their owners, and walk out again unseen, taking nothing. All through the long ride back from the city she had been glancing furtively at half a dozen pressing motives, possessed by half a dozen well-known, well-loved people.

"Whoever did it," Lee remarked, "made particularly certain that Denis Cotton should be the first suspect."

So he was not sure, and Denis was not yet under arrest. He intercepted the relieved glance she gave him and made haste to cover the admission.

"Young chaps with that kind of war experience are often insanely reckless," he remarked.

"Perhaps they are," she agreed, "but it wouldn't make them fools, would it? I mean, by French law the one thing which can prevent a legal heir inheriting is his conviction of murdering the deceased."

Lee sat back. "So you knew that?"

"Not unnaturally. I am French. I wondered if you knew it. It seems rather important."

He did not reply to that, but she saw that it was one of the pieces of information he had gathered. It explained some of his uncertainty.

His next question did succeed in surprising her.

"Would you say Mr. Cotton knew a great deal about jewels?"

"About jewels?"

"Yes. Would he understand their value? Know if they were good or bad?"

She sat frowning at him, looking for some catch in the question, and it struck him again how remarkably beautiful she was. It set him wondering how much there was in the story of the sudden love affair between her and the tough young doctor whom he had liked despite himself. The youngster had appeared to adore her. He wondered if she was playing with the fellow after all. He didn't know.

"Do you mean stage jewellery?" she said. "Or just bad taste?"

Lee came out of his thoughts with a start.

"Madame Zoffany had some stage jewellery, had she?" he said with some interest.

"She had everything. Some of it was lovely. Some of it was—well, just stage jewellery."

He opened a drawer in the desk and drew out a large jewel-studded cross, which he carried over to her.

"What would you call this?"

She hardly glanced at it. "It's old French paste. Very nice but not frightfully valuable. Zoff wore it when she played Tosca. She kept it as a souvenir. I've borrowed it once or twice for costume parts."

"Thank you." He put the cross back in the desk. "Would Mr. Cotton know that?"

Margot raised weary eyes to his face.

"I should think anyone could see they aren't diamonds, if that's what you mean," she said.

He nodded regretfully. "All right," he said abruptly. "We'll just have the formal statement, and that'll be all for the time being."

He touched a buzzer, destroying the fiction that the stenographer's absence was accidental. Before the bell was answered the phone trilled and he pounced upon it.

"Brandt? Lee here. What?" Astonishment spread over his face as he listened. "Good lord," he said at last, and then again, "good lord. Where did you say? In the where? Spell it. Yes, that's what I thought you said. All right, I'll come at once. Quite. I agree. Alters things quite a bit. Good-bye."

He hung up slowly. The solid flesh on his forehead was drawn up into tight folds and the incoming secretary was met with a blank stare before he relaxed.

"No," he said to the man. "No, after all I shan't bother. That'll do, Miss Robert. Thank you for your co-operation."

She rose uncertainly. "Do you mean I can go?"

"As soon as you like. I'd prefer you to stay at Clough House for a little, though. I'll take you down with me."

"And Denis?"

A curious expression passed over the heavy red face.

"I suppose Mr. Cotton had better come too," he said thoughtfully.

However, in the end she did not go back with him
after all. There were brief apologies without explanations, and he and the superintendent of the county
police went on ahead, taking Denis with them, while she
was left to be driven home in lesser state by a police
sergeant.

Altogether the delay was considerable. She did not
see Denis and was grateful. She had taken Lee's thrust
without wincing rather than parrying it, and the pain
came later. While she waited for her driver she had
time to remember, and several points returned to her
with uncomfortable clarity. Principal among them was
the fact that the impetus in her love affair with Denis
was her own. Last night, in Zoff's drawing room, she
had been deliriously happy to discover that she was
loved. Today, in the dingy waiting room in Dower
Street, it had been reaffirmed. And yet it was true that
on each occasion there had been considerable resistance, which she had put down to outside causes. In
her present mood it was very easy for her to underestimate Lee and to be convinced that he could only have
got the ugly word "infatuation" from someone else.
There was only one other person who could have put it
into his mind.

They took her back to Zoff's house at last. She sat in a
very small car beside a very large sergeant who drove
as if he were taking a safety test. The streets were
deserted and it was very cool, with an irritable wind
flickering over the roofs of the neat little houses hud-
dling together under a bright starlit sky.

At the first glimpse of the familiar gates in the
headlights she was surprised by the crowd before them.
It was not very big but it was characteristic and would
grow. Placid, stupid faces on nondescript forms stood
patiently, gaping at the light showing through curtained
windows which revealed nothing. Before them, barring
the way, was the gleam of silver on blue serge.

The drive was crowded with vehicles already, and

they edged their way in behind a small black van whose significance did not occur to the girl.

Her escort, having safely delivered her, seemed loth to depart.

"I'll take you into the hall," he said. "That'll be about right. You lead the way, miss."

She got out of the car feeling small and cold. Her legs were trembling. The lights in the conservatory porch were on and she stepped into it, to pause in astonishment. An unexpected figure was advancing toward her across it. The man was unmistakable. His air of respectability, overlaid with dubious magnificence, seedy black overcoat, shining silk hat, added up to undertaker's mute as surely as two and two to four. Yet it was nighttime and Zoff had only been dead a few hours. By no possible twist of circumstance could her funeral be taking place now.

He gave her an inquisitive once-over and glanced behind him, where, to her relief, she caught sight of Sir Kit's plump back in the entrance. He was watching something in the hall but swung round as she touched his arm.

"Oh, Margot!" he said and caught hold of her.

In the last few hours he had grown old. His hands were trembling violently and the plump pouches of his cheeks had sagged.

"Good God, eh! Good God!" he exploded. "D'you know, Margot, they were going to send her down into the town in a public mortuary van? I couldn't have that, could I? I've been moving heaven and earth to get them to show a little decency. Proper respect, eh? Proper respect for our dear girl."

His tired old voice was strained and she had a momentary terror that she must hear it break. She recognised his mood with dismay. He was beside himself with grief and shock and was clinging to the conventions as a man clings to a spar in a torrent. Obviously he saw nothing ludicrous in the outburst and now waved a hand at the scene before him in a gesture which was helpless and pathetic.

"Done all I can," he said. "It isn't much."

She followed his eyes to a picture which had all the degrading absurdity which so often surrounds things genuinely tragic.

At the foot of the staircase, and advancing toward them, was an embarrassed procession. Two mortuary attendants, holding their caps under their arms, a method clearly both new and inconvenient, carried between them a regulation stretcher. Upon it, under the regulation blanket, was something still and horrible. But over the blanket, partially hiding it, trailed one of Zoff's own white Chinese shawls, its heavy fringe threatening to trip the bearers at every step.

On either side of the main group walked two undertaker's men. All were uncomfortable and very uncertain of the etiquette of the occasion. One of them carried the sheaf of roses which Zoff herself had presented to Margot the evening before. They had been standing in a bowl on a chest in the landing and now dripped water through the black woollen gloves clasping them. A trail of it made a bright cascade down the man's shabby overcoat.

A plain-clothes detective standing in the drawing-room doorway eyed the scene with grim irritation but made no effort to interfere. Sir Kit beckoned the cortege on.

"The police have been very kind," he said to Margot. "I got on to old Forsyte, the chief constable. I know him slightly and I think he put in a word for me. They want a post-mortem, you see. Have to do their duty, I know that, but I've made 'em show a little respect."

He was blethering, letting it all rush out without any ordered thought, and Margot felt her eyes filling; not for Zoff, who would assuredly be laughing at the whole sorry performance, but for him whose loss was so achingly apparent.

"I made the undertaker send these fellows," he said.

"He didn't want to. Seemed to think I was mad. But she couldn't go out of this house like a—a parcel, Margot." His voice trembled again but he controlled it. The procession was passing them now and he prepared to follow it.

The senior mute, who had been waiting in the hall, came over to him.

"I shouldn't come, sir," he said, revealing a kindly cockney voice. "You go and sit down and leave it to us. You won't do a mite o' good. You stay at 'ome with the young lady."

"No, Kit, don't go with them." Margot had no clear idea of the grisly programme ahead but she felt most strongly that he should not be there.

He took her hand gently from his sleeve.

"I shall go," he said with all his old authority. "Don't try to stop me, my dear. I shall see the last of her. She'd like that."

His voice broke utterly and became a whisper.

"You stay here and be a good girl until I come back."

There was no more to be said after that. The undertaker's man shook his head disapprovingly but made no more protest, and Kit went quietly out into the dark drive. Margot turned slowly back into the house and walked toward the staircase.

Her one desire was to throw herself on her bed, and her foot was on the lowest step when the plain-clothes man reached her.

"Not upstairs, miss, if you please," he said firmly. "The inspector left orders that no one at all was to go up. You're Miss Robert, aren't you?"

"Yes."

"I thought so. I'm not sure if you're wanted. Will you come in here for a minute?"

He took her into the drawing room, where one of the card tables had been pulled out into the centre of the room. A constable in uniform sat at it, an ink pad and paper spread out before him. The room was in disorder. All the furniture surrounding the broken clock had been pulled back. Its gilt extravagance brought Zoff to mind so vividly that she caught her breath.

Her escort was whispering to the man at the table, who looked at her dubiously over a pair of pince-nez.

"No," he said in a booming voice of great affability. "No, I don't think we need bother you, miss. There were no instructions left about getting your prints. We've took all we need, I think."

"Fingerprints?" she said in surprise. There was no reason, of course, why they should not take them, but the idea shocked her.

"Yes, miss, fingerprints." He appeared to relish the word. "Just them we wanted. Nothing to worry you with."

"Then I can go where I like, can I?"

"Anywhere except upstairs." They spoke in unison and appeared to find the accident amusing, for they grinned surreptitiously at each other like boys in church.

Margot was overcome with a hatred of them all. Lee and his hosts were enemies in the house, silly, excited, overinterested enemies. The colour came into her face and she turned on her heel and went out. The constable looked at his colleague and turned his thumbs up approvingly, but he was a discreet man and made no other comment.

Margot went along to the dining room. The house was unnaturally silent and yet she was aware of activity going on in its recesses. The atmosphere was oppressive, as though the very air tingled. Somewhere, surely, some sort of family council must be taking place? If so, she was anxious to join it. She saw hopefully that the dining-room lights were on and the air struck warm as she entered, but the only sounds were not those of conversation.

The single occupant lay in the winged chair before the remains of a fire. Victor Soubise was snoring deeply, flushed face half hidden in the crook of his arm, his thin legs sprawled out across the rug. She stared at him in astonishment and had a hand on his shoulder before the reek of brandy reached her. He grunted and muttered something but did not wake, and she stepped back, her glance falling on the low table by his side.

A solid spirit decanter stood empty and stopperless in a puddle on the polished wood. By its side was a tumbler, in which there was still half an inch or so of neat spirits. Exasperation spread over her. The decanter was usually kept three parts full at least, and unless something extraordinary had occurred Victor must have swallowed the best part of a pint. Obviously there was no point in trying to wake him. He would remain in that state for some time.

She left him and went back down the corridor, her heels clicking angrily on the tiles. She was furious with him. In the ordinary way he was an abstemious, slightly maidenly sort of person about alcohol who considered himself something of a connoisseur. An exhibition of this sort from anyone else would have brought a very sour little smile to his face.

Margot had known him all her life and had seen him in times of crisis before, when his behaviour had been fussy rather than unco-operative. Yet now she was so shaken and so angry with him for putting himself out of action at the time when he might have been useful that she did not stop to consider what an extraordinary and untypical thing it was for him to do.

# EIGHT

Margot stood hesitating at the top of the service stairs. At first she thought the kitchen was deserted, but presently, as homely as a voice, the clatter of crockery came floating up to her.

Genevieve was at the table in her best black dress. It was far too tight for her round the hips and had ruckled up at the back, to show some inches of plaid petticoat, but the tuckers at her throat and wrists were white and crisp. To save it she had put on her cooking apron, a vast affair of red-and-white gingham, and, together with her little black head shawl, her appearance suggested festivity, not to say fancy dress. Only her face was tragic. She had not been crying; the black eyes were as clear and bright as ever, but the wrinkles had multiplied and there was pallor under her brown skin.

The moment she caught sight of Margot she put a finger to her lips and crept softly over to the door which led out into a small back hall, off which Felix had a bedroom. She listened against it for a moment before opening it cautiously. A glance satisfied her and she came back.

"They are everywhere, the *sales types*," she said, her voice lowered to a whisper of startling vituperation. "Now what is the matter with you? You look as if you were in consumption. Sit down, child, and take off that hat. It is disrespectful at such a time. We'll have some coffee."

Her plump hands belied the brusqueness of the words. She pulled out a chair and sat the girl in it, patting her shoulder as she passed.

"If Madame were here, we should be eating," she went on. "This is the moment for a good *jambon* and a conserve of walnut. If the world were not demented, we should have both. Madame always said that a full stomach knows no broken heart. We will prove her right, eh, *petite* Margot?"

She was frowning tremendously and the girl recognised the symptoms. Genevieve was both frightened and angry and was taking refuge in ferocity. Grief was yet to come. Margot found her comforting. This performance had the virtue of familiarity. Genevieve, at any rate, was still recognisable.

She bustled about, rattling the glowing copper on the charcoal stove as if it had offended her, but she was waiting for the question when it came.

"They've found something. What is it?"

The old woman pursed up her lips as if she were about to spit and turned round, coffeepot in hand.

"Nothing that I could not have told them in the first ten minutes, had they had the sense to ask," she said. "We all knew of the little cupboard in the carving of the bed head. It was not secret. Madame kept *sal volatile* there, and later the little pellecules the doctor gave her for her heart. Yet when Felix remembered it and opened it, the ridiculous *flic* left in charge while *monsieur l'inspecteur* was away made a performance to astonish one."

The cupboard in the bed head. Margot remembered it. It was linked with her childhood. It was Zoff's pet hiding place, and it had yielded her a thousand sugared almonds in the days when they were still all in Paris. Always when Genevieve brought her in at eleven o'clock to receive Zoff's morning kiss the little cupboard, cunningly hidden behind a knot of golden cupids, would swing open and out would come the familiar blue-and-gold carton from De Bry.

"What did they find?"

"Eh?" Genevieve was uneasy. Her glance, curiously direct, rested on the girl. "*Chérie,*" she said, "they found the diamonds, the emerald collar, all the pearls, and a bottle."

"How d'you mean, a bottle? What of?"

"Of chloroform, *petite.* It has been lying about the house these two years, as I could have told them, as I tried to tell them. But they were so important and so engaged that they could not spare the time to listen."

The room was fragrant with coffee by this time, and she placed a smoking bowl of it on the white boards before the girl. Margot waved it away.

"I don't understand this, Gen'vieve," she said. "Why was it lying about, as you call it? Why was it ever in the house?"

"My God, for the flies, of course." The old lady was growing sulky. "Drink up your good coffee. There is cream from the top of the milk upon it. Since the war has ended there has been a new spray for the flies, but in the war, when you were in the north that summer,

there was nothing, and Sir Kit, poor man, was at his
wit's end to know how to clear the place of them for
Madame. She had one of her moods, you understand."

She paused and spread out her hands.

"Actually there were few of them, but they worried
Madame and she sent for Sir Kit and complained. He
took her advice and one day a man came and we shut
up all the rooms and they were sprayed with chloroform. Some of it was left in the bottle. It used to stand
on a shelf in the little glass pantry at the top of these
back stairs. It was there always. I had not missed it."

"But, darling, do you realise what you're saying?"
Margot was sitting up in the chair, her fair hair tousled,
her eyes horrified. "Everyone in the house must have
known of this, Sir Kit too."

"Certainly Sir Kit." Genevieve's little grunt was near
laughter. "That is what the so intelligent *flics* have
discovered. We all knew of the little cupboard, we all
knew of the chloroform."

"Except me."

"You knew of the cupboard, *ma mie*, and I am
surprised you had not heard of the chloroform. Certainly Monsieur Victor knew, because he was discussing the
new spray with me only the other day and I told him it
was far better than the old. We were in the pantry at
the time."

"But Denis——"

"No." The old woman leaned across the table and
pushed the coffee toward her. "No. Monsieur Denis
could not have known, either of the cupboard or of the
spray. That is why he is not yet under arrest. They have
taken him upstairs."

Margot passed her hand wearily over her forehead.

"Oh, Gen'vieve," she said huskily, "who—who is it?"

"I do not know." The old voice was unexpectedly
vigorous. "Not yet." She hesitated and added gently:
"*Pauvre femme*, she made people so enraged. There
were times when I, even I, her *bonne*, who loved her,
I could have killed her almost."

"Whom do they suspect now?"

"Felix," said Genevieve calmly. "They are not men of imagination." She began to cut bread and butter very neatly, setting each piece tastefully over the other on a plate to make a design.

"Felix?"

"*Oui*, because of the clock. Felix broke the clock. Oh, but I knew that immediately I saw it last night. But they have been smearing the house with powder and our fingers with ink, like lunatics, and they discovered it too in the end. Such a fuss! The clockmaker would not touch it last night, you know. He took one look at it and said to mend it was impossible, so the story was clear for them to read."

Margot remained watching her busy hands in shocked astonishment.

"He was trying to take some sort of revenge, I suppose," she murmured.

"Naturally." Genevieve was content. "Felix has been making a fool of himself for years, worrying over what? —the eleventh share of a baker's shop which was never out of debt."

"How do you know he did it?"

"Because, *petite*"—Genevieve pointed her statement with the bread knife—"because there was no one else who could have done it. That is always the answer. Sometimes one refuses to see it, but in the end that is the explanation. There are no miracles in these matters. The one who is left is the one who is guilty. You will see, it will arrive that way in this more terrible affair."

"I hope so. I don't think I can bear much more of this, Gen'vieve. Where is Felix now?"

"In his bedroom, with yet another detective." She was grimly amused. "Serve him right to suffer a little. He's beside himself, the miserable recreant. He hoped to kill Madame."

"Gen'vieve! What are you saying?"

"The truth. The truth before the Blessed Virgin

and all the saints. He knew the clock was her mascot and he hoped the shock would give her a heart attack and she would die. Then he could go and grovel in the flour sweepings for his contemptible inheritance. He did not know that Madame's heart was very nearly as strong as mine."

She was talking very fast and at the top of her voice.

"That is the sort of murderer we have in the poor Felix. The wishful one, who dreams, but whose hand trembles so he cuts his own finger with the dagger. He dared not hurt her and so he broke the clock. When he was found out he thought they would suspect him of the chloroform also. *Mon Dieu*, what an animal! I would not look at him when they brought him through. I hope he suffered."

"That sounds charitable, Gen'vieve. I hope you're not talking about me."

The voice from the doorway surprised them both. Margot's hand shook so violently that some of the coffee was spilt on the scrubbed board. Genevieve reached for a tea towel to mop it before she glanced up. She spoke amicably if directly.

"Good evening, Monsieur Denis. One can see you have not been listening at the door or you would know we were not discussing you."

He remained on the threshold, watching them. He was still white and tired-looking, but the nervous tension had gone out of his face.

"I smell coffee," he said. "I'm afraid the sleuths want you, Gen'vieve. I said I'd find you."

"Again?" She sounded exasperated, but she passed her tongue across her narrow lips and her eyes were uneasy. "Very well, I will go up to them. Margot, the coffee is there, the milk is there, the sugar is rationed."

She trundled across the kitchen, pausing to flick her head shawl into position as she passed the spotted mirror on the wall. Denis held the door for her and they heard her heavy feet shaking the stairs as she mounted them. He shut the door and came in while Margot crossed to the dresser to fetch a third bowl.

"D'you mind one of these?" she enquired. "Or do you want a cup?"

"I'll have it in anything, please," he said, seating himself at the table and resting his elbows heavily upon it. "What's the matter with *you*?"

The light reflected from the copper pot made little flecks of orange in her eyes.

"I'm tired."

"So am I. But I don't radiate ice waves. Has that perishing policeman been sowing evil seeds?"

"No."

"Good." He took the bowl from her hands and sipped some of the scalding stuff. "I rather thought he might. His methods are ingenious but not quite clever enough, I thought. Strike you that way?"

"I don't know. I didn't notice."

He looked up sharply, his eyes meeting hers.

"Margot," he said gravely, "I had the hell of a row with Zoff after *déjeuner* today. She came down and fetched me out of the dining room, where I had my meal alone. We had a most violent showdown up in her room. In fact, we've been quarrelling for quite a long time, some months."

She put up a hand to stop him, but he ignored it.

"I want you to listen to this, and we haven't a lot of time. You've got to understand my side of the story. When you were out of the country Zoff wrote to me at St. Mark's. I haven't kept the letter, so I can't show it to the police, but you must take my word for it. She asked me to come down one week end, and when she got me here she dragged out all that stuff about my mother not being her daughter, all the horrible old dirty linen which was washed out in the Paris courts when I was in arms. She wanted me to take a lump sum in cash and repudiate my inheritance. She offered me a few million francs—

about twelve thousand dollars, something like that. I laughed at her, I'm afraid, and I thought the matter was finished."

He was still holding her glance, appealing to her to understand him, but she dragged her eyes away from him. The story could well be true, but she did not want to hear any more.

"Then she had another shot," he went on relentlessly, "and in the end she made me interested. It was all very secret, between ourselves, you understand. But she seemed to know how my mind works and she got me guessing. Finally I said that if she'd prove to me that she was right I'd step out, as I didn't want any money that wasn't mine. Well, she was always going to produce this proof and she never did. When I approached her she would put me off and just raise her original offer a thousand dollars or so. Margot, are you listening to me?"

She nodded without speaking, but she did not look at him. She knew as well as anybody how infuriating Zoff could be and she was beginning to be dreadfully afraid. She had never seen Denis in a rage but she could believe that it would be formidable. There was a recklessness about him now which reminded her frighteningly of something Lee had said about him, and she was afraid to hear what he seemed so determined to tell her.

"I won't repeat the tricks she got up to," he was saying, his voice harsh with the effort of control. "That setout last night was only one of them. I told her I was coming to see her, and she said she'd send for the police and charge me with attempting to murder her. I laughed, and she did do just that. It startled me because I thought she must be crazy and I didn't mean to go up. But as I told you, when Victor and Sir Kit went out she came down herself in a house gown and told me to come up to her room as she had something to show me."

He paused and Margot forced herself to look into his white face.

"The thing she gave me was that old green bag," he went on deliberately. "She said the proofs were in it and that I was to take them home and study them. I opened it in front of her and saw that it was full of papers. The thing I didn't do was to look in that drawer affair at the bottom. I didn't see that until I was in the train."

"Then you didn't know about the jewellery?"

"Of course I didn't!" he exploded. "And when I did find it I made an idiotic mistake. I'm no expert, and at first sight the stuff was impressive. I assumed she was trying to bribe me. Now I feel certain that the inspector is right, and that since the wretched stuff is not particularly valuable she had merely forgotten it was there. At the time I thought the worst and I was pretty angry. I took the documents and bunged the bag and its contents in a station cloakroom. Now her real and valuable stuff has been found in her room, in a secret hiding place in the bed if you please! She was an extraordinary person, Margot."

The girl did not stir. She was waiting for the rest. He was beginning to show reluctance. She wanted to hear and yet could hardly bear it.

"Her proofs were nothing but cuttings from the French press at the time of the case," he went on bitterly. "I was looking at them when you arrived in Dower Street. That was why I was so furious I could hardly speak to you."

She scarcely heard him. Her attention was still focused in fascinated apprehension on the main part of his story.

"When was the quarrel?" she asked slowly. "When she gave you the bag?"

"No," he said briefly. "No, before then."

There was a long silence while they sat opposite one another, the gay colours of china and metal on the dressers behind them contrasting with the pallor of their faces.

"Was it about me?"

"Oh, she had had a shot at you first I suppose." He was suspicious and the colour came flooding back into his face darkening his eyes and accentuating the anger there.

"No, it wasn't that. But I know Zoff. I think I can guess what she said."

"I hope you can't," he objected grimly. "There was spite in it, something I can hardly describe. It was as if she felt she was being revenged on me and that's ridiculous, for God knows I've never done her any harm."

Margot's imagination painted the scene which must have taken place. She could hear Zoff accusing him of hunting a second fortune since he was not sure of the first. She knew from experience that there was nothing, absolutely nothing, that Zoff would not say, no line that she would feel bound to draw. Margot could imagine any man's anger turning to fury under that vituperative tongue. The questions forcing themselves before her became terrible. Just exactly how angry had he been? What was he about to confess to her now?

She glanced at him nervously. God knew he did not look like the murderer of an old woman. And yet there was recklessness there and deeply wounded pride. Her faith in him wavered helplessly.

He spoke again, still holding her eyes.

"She also made it clear to me that it would be criminal of me to expect you to marry me. I had not realised what the career of a great actress entails, or even that you were one, I'm afraid."

"I'm not," she protested. "At least, I don't think so. Zoff exaggerated. She was so anxious for her success to continue, you see. She——"

"I've got work I must do," he went on, cutting across her objections as if he were determined not to hear them. "It's waiting and it's just got to be done. I can't go wandering round the capitals of Europe in your entourage. When she put it so brutally, I saw it. That was why I cleared out when I did. I think it made me a little crazy at the time. I just took the damned bag and went. I couldn't face you after——"

He broke off halfway through the sentence, recognising suddenly the pure terror in her eyes.

"Margot, you don't believe that I'm telling you . . ." He pushed back his chair so violently that it fell with a clatter, and he came round the room to put both hands on her shoulders. "Look here, get this straight at once. I'm not trying to tell you that I killed Zoff. That's what you're thinking, aren't you?"

The rattling of the handle of the inner door sounded like a thunderclap. She thrust him away from her and sprang up just as a pink-faced young plain-clothes man, whom neither of them had seen before, emerged from the inner hall. He glanced from one to the other with inquisitive eyes, and his hands, which stuck out a little too far from the sleeves of his tightly buttoned coat, were crimson and cold-looking.

"I've got the French chap who works here in his room out the back," he began awkwardly. "He doesn't seem too good, and as I smelled coffee I wondered if a cup might help him. Cheer him up like."

Margot did not look at Denis directly but she was wretchedly aware of the new bitterness in his eyes.

"Yes, of course," she said to the newcomer, who was still gangling hopefully in the doorway. "I'll make some more. You'd like some yourself, I expect?"

"It wouldn't come amiss." The pink face brightened. "I've been here since dinnertime and it's cold out there. The old chap's got the horribles. It makes you feel perished to look at him. I hope I didn't interrupt you." He paused and hunted for a more conciliatory suggestion. "Talking, or anything."

"Not at all." Denis spoke briefly and handed Margot the coffeepot.

"I'm glad of that," said the youngster, who seemed

destined to be a social failure. "I'll get the cups. These green 'uns here?"

"No, *mon Dieu*, no! Whatever next?"

Genevieve, entering like a tug from the other door, embraced the situation in one comprehensive glance, and the fingers of the plain-clothes man shrivelled away from the porcelain.

"I will attend to it," she announced. "Mademoiselle, that is not the canister I am using. You will all sit down, if you please, and leave it to me."

She was breathless and more truculent than ever, and as she bore down upon the stove she glanced spitefully at Denis.

"I am an old woman, and you send me upstairs for nothing, for nothing at all," she said accusingly. "All the same, I made good use of my time. They know now where they get away, these wretched inspectors."

A slow smile spread over the shining face of the detective.

"She means 'off'," he observed happily. "You told 'em where they got off, did you, Ma? That shook 'em, I daresay."

Genevieve, kettle in hand, favoured him with a stare which had quelled greater men. He looked hurt.

"Sorry, I'm sure," he said.

She ignored him and took down two coarse white cups, while they watched her in silence.

"There," she said at last as she filled them and stood back. "Carry them carefully, young man. I do not wish to clean the floor tonight."

"Don't you worry, ducks." The youngster grinned at her. "Leave it to Skinner. Skinner's a tidy bloke, Skinner is. Learned it in the Army. Well, thanks one and all."

His good humour was comforting. Genevieve relented sufficiently to open the door for him, and they saw his narrow back held stiffly as he edged across the flags to the bedroom, the cups rattling faintly in his thick hands.

178

They were just turning away when the crash came and they heard his cry. Denis crossed the narrow hall in a stride, with Margot behind him. By the time Genevieve reached them they were in the room and her explosion of rage at the broken cups and spilled coffee died abruptly.

In the centre of a sordid room, which was cold and yet stuffy, Denis was supporting a writhing figure hardly recognisable as Felix. He was hanging from an old lamp hook in the ceiling, an overturned chair at his feet. As Genevieve screamed, the detective slashed the length of pajama cord which had been looped round his neck and Denis carried him, still kicking, to the bed.

## NINE

It was Lee who made the decision to see them all together, to thrash out the whole thing once and for all. It was his case anyhow, and already the press were at his heels, liable at any moment to start screaming for Scotland Yard intervention.

The county superintendent, who was a heavy, white-faced man a few months off the retiring age, was against the idea, naturally, on grounds of unorthodoxy, but he had his own private reasons, connected with a wife in hospital down at Bray, for wanting to see the business over in record time. Also, of course, it was not entirely his affair. The borough police were in charge, and if things went badly wrong, so that the story came out in headlines, Lee would take most of the rap.

The inspector made up his mind in the bedroom where Felix lay. The old man was more frightened than hurt, save for a swollen tongue and a bruised larynx. He could talk, and what he said was fairly convincing. Lee listened to him for a time and then came storming into the kitchen, where the original trio still waited, to tell them what he wanted.

To Margot he looked like a caricature of a policeman

179

as he loomed in the doorway issuing orders. He was an
outsize man, and in the thick black overcoat he had
never had time to remove since he entered the house
he seemed to fill half the kitchen. His fleshy face was
now almost purple and brute energy radiated from it.

"Upstairs," he said. "In that bedroom where it
happened. By that merry-go-round of a bed. We'll go
through the whole thing there and we'll get it washed
up if it takes a week. There's half a dozen of you could
have done it, and most with good motives as far as I can
see, and I'm going to wring it out of you if it sends us
all to the squirrel's cage."

The old super coughed deprecatingly at this point,
and Lee's small eyes slid sideways at him and back
again.

"It's all very well," he said. "But if a man tries to kill
himself because he busted a clock which was supposed
to be lucky, it makes one wonder what sort of setup
there was round here before the old lady died."

At Margot's side Genevieve stirred. She had been
simmering quietly for some time.

"Felix could not have killed Madame. He was here
with me until we heard Monsieur Denis come downstairs. Then we went out together and saw him come
out with Madame's case."

"That's right," said Lee, "unless you were both in it.
Everybody upstairs, please."

He swung round on the unlucky Skinner, who looked
like a before-treatment picture of himself as he wilted
in a corner.

"You bring the old man," he said, "and if he looks
groggy, don't rush out for coffee."

They trooped upstairs, all as angry as Lee had hoped
to make them.

Zoff's room looked more vast and more dated than
ever before. With the passing of her personality all the
tawdriness of the stage, and the genuine but outmoded
elegance with which she had surrounded herself, lay
stark without glamour. For the first time one saw that

the room had belonged to an old woman. The bed was dismantled. Peach satin and blue quilted silk trailed on the carpet, while the small cupboard behind the cupids on the headboard stood open and empty. It looked dusty inside and as if there might be hairpins lying there.

The inquisition did not start immediately, but Lee did not leave them alone. The two detectives from the drawing room followed them up and stood about in an ostentatious attempt to be self-effacing. When addressed, they pretended somehow to be too polite to answer.

Genevieve waddled down the room and seated herself on one of the more extraordinary pieces of furniture it contained. This was an old circular ottoman with a solid pear-shaped cushion in the centre. Zoff had had it quilted and buttoned in blue satin. The old woman balanced on the rim of it, looking like a black prune on a blue plate.

Denis followed Margot to the centre window. He had not left her side since that moment of crisis between them, but even now they were not allowed to talk. One of the detectives wandered casually to within a few feet of them and stood staring earnestly at the row of finely bound French plays which filled a case on the wall near by.

Sir Kit came in next. He appeared in the doorway, looking shrunken but much less lost than when the girl had seen him last. He came over to her at once, nodding at Denis as he passed.

"This is a monstrous imposition, but on the whole a wise move, I think," he announced unexpectedly. "I met the inspector as I came in just now. I don't like the feller's manner, but he's sincere, I think, and determined to do his job. Not bad traits at a time like this."

Margot eyed him curiously. He was more normal than usual. The moment of despair was over, evidently, and he had a grip on himself even if for the time being he was inclined to overplay the part. She asked no questions lest she should overbalance him again, but after a pause he bent close to her.

"They wouldn't let me go in," he whispered. "Very kindly fellers, you know. Meant well. But remarkably firm. Perhaps it was as well. I saw her to the door."

The old-fashioned phrase struck his own ears as unhappy, and his lips quirked bitterly.

"Now who are we waiting for?" he demanded. "Victor? Felix?"

The door, opening at that moment, silenced him. Lee appeared, followed by the superintendent, and after them Victor Soubise. He was steady on his feet but grey round the gills, and his hair was recently wet. He did not look at anybody, but sank down in a gilt armchair not far inside the room and remained looking at his fingertips, his paper-fine lids, which were so like Zoff's own, drawn down over his eyes.

Margot watched him for a moment or two and was turning back when she caught Sir Kit's expression. It surprised her. It was a curious look to find in those kindly eyes, speculative, cold and apprehensive.

Her attention was diverted by the two last arrivals. Skinner came in, supporting the tottering Felix. The old man was ghastly. His bones were wrapped in a dirty plaid dressing gown, and a woollen scarf emphasised rather than hid the wads of cotton wool which surrounded his grey face like a ruff. All the same he was still very much alive. He had been cut down within a couple of seconds of his kicking away the chair and, though badly shocked, was recovering rapidly. Sir Kit made little teetering sounds of disapproval.

"Damnable to submit a man in that condition to an ordeal like this," he murmured. "You're a doctor, Denis. What do you say?"

The younger man gave the forlorn exhibit a long glance from under his lashes.

"I've seen men in worse shape submitted to more," he whispered drily. "I think he'll do. It won't kill him. Soubise looks in a mess."

"Ah," said Sir Kit. He spoke aloud, forgetting where they were, and had to cough to cover it.

As if the sound were a signal, Lee, who had been sitting in the chair at the end of the bed, glanced up from a page of notes in his hand and rose to his feet. He stood looking round at them for some time, his eyes gleaming with a knowingness which was intentionally offensive.

"There's been a murder done," he said. The statement was meant to be shocking and succeeded, although there was no news in it.

Sir Kit grew slowly crimson and Genevieve's intake of breath was audible in the silence.

"Somebody did it," said Lee. "We don't want to forget that, do we?"

He let that sink in and went on, still speaking as if they were younger and more stupid than himself, but all the time the light in his eyes and the way they flickered from one face to another proclaimed the fact that he did not really believe they were any of them obtuse or negligible. Margot found him terrible. There was no humanity in him. He was not thinking of himself. He was simply a machine for finding out.

"The dead woman was a stranger to me," he said. "You're all strangers to me and the superintendent, and perhaps for that reason we see things a bit plainer than some of you do. Now I'm going to tell you some of the details we know, and I think you'll be able to fill in the gaps for us. You're listening, aren't you?"

Of course they were listening. Kit was on the verge of saying so forcibly, but he too was beginning to see something of Lee's methods and forced himself to keep his temper and silence.

"The first thing that happened, as far as I'm concerned, was yesterday," Lee went on. "The deceased applied for police protection against her grandson Denis Cotton. A few hours later she withdrew the charge. That was after she had had an interview with her ward, Margot Robert."

He paused, and looked at Margot and Denis until everyone in the room had noted that they were standing side by side.

"The second thing that happened was this afternoon at three-forty. The deceased's doctor telephoned the station to tell me that he had been summoned by Genevieve Lestrade and Felix Monet, servants of the deceased, and had come to the house to discover Margot Robert on the doorstep with a friend of hers called Hercule Bonnet. Some seconds later he found his patient dead in bed, poisoned by chloroform inhaled. There was no trace of a bottle or container which might have held this liquid in the room so far as he could ascertain."

He coughed and consulted his notes.

"The doctor stated that in his opinion the woman had been dead for something less than one hour. This opinion was subsequently confirmed by the police surgeon. For clarity's sake we will place the time of death at approximately two-thirty."

He glanced at the superintendent for confirmation, and the older man nodded, although his expression remained uneasy. Lee continued, blithely confident.

"The doctor also said that the two servants had deposed that they went up to their mistress immediately after they had seen Denis Cotton descend the staircase and go out of the house carrying her jewel case. I asked him if Margot Robert was still in the house and he gave me to understand that she was."

Again he let the point sink in.

"After taking certain steps, I came to this house and made certain investigations, and later, on receiving information from one of my subordinates, I went to 125 Dower Street, London W.C.1., where I found Denis Cotton and Margot Robert together, she having slipped out unbeknownst to anyone in this house. Denis Cotton admitted possession of the jewel case and it was subsequently recovered. I then brought both these persons to the Bridgewyck police station."

He managed to convey police omnipotence very neatly and sailed on, rolling out the damning story without apparent enmity.

"While they were still at the station I received a telephone call from Sergeant Brandt, to tell me that Felix Monet, who had been assisting the police to estimate what valuables might have been taken from the house, had remembered a small cupboard built into the headboard of the deceased's bed. You will see it directly behind me."

His manner, if irritating, was also compelling. Obediently everyone looked toward the hiding place. Denis's glance alone fumbled for a second before it lighted upon the dusty little cavern. His eyebrows rose slightly as he discovered it, but he looked away at once, and Lee, who was watching him, smiled. There was no telling if he were congratulating himself on the working out of a theory, or Denis on trying to be subtle.

"That cupboard," Lee continued, "contained a twelve-ounce bottle in which a drain of chloroform remained, and also all the more valuable pieces of jewellery which Madame Zoffany possessed, some of it, I am told, worth many thousands of pounds. It was discovered in the presence of the sergeant by Felix Monet."

Sir Kit touched Margot's arm. He looked completely bewildered. Before he could speak, however, Lee, whose eyes seemed to be everywhere, pounced on him.

"I am about to explain, Sir Christopher," he put in quickly, "that the green case which Denis Cotton took to London has now been found to contain a great many ornaments of what I shall call secondary value, ornaments of a kind used on the stage. They were secreted in this false bottom of the case, and there is some question as to whether or not they were put there by mistake and the bag used to carry something else. Denis Cotton has made a statement to the effect that he did not know they were there when he carried the bag from the house. Now, there are two other people

185

concerned in this enquiry: Sir Christopher Perrins and Victor Soubise."

Kit nodded, but Victor did not raise his eyes.

"On their two statements, each taken separately, of course"—Lee still sounded very pleased with himself—"they left the house together about eleven forty-five in the morning and went down into the town, where it is certain that they had lunch together at the Conservative Club. They left at approximately one forty-five and walked back toward the house, still in company."

His voice ceased and there was silence in the room, during which Margot was suddenly acutely aware of Zoff's personality. It was as vivid as if she had entered the room and was standing there just behind the inspector. The girl shook off the horrible fantasy. The startling recollection of the indomitable woman remained in her mind. This was Drama: Zoff would have liked this.

"They did not enter the front door," Lee was saying "but came in at the garden gate, as Sir Christopher wished to look at the small greenhouse at the end of the lawn. He went in, he says, and remained there for a considerable period inspecting the plants and also examining the heating arrangements, which have fallen into disrepair. Soubise left him and came into the house by the side door. On his own deposition he went into the dining room, poured himself a drink, and then went up to his room, where he collected some documents which he wished to show Sir Christopher. It took him some minutes to find these, and he came out of the house by the way he had entered it at approximately two twenty-five, having encountered no one. He and Sir Christopher then went for a short walk together to visit a jobbing clockmaker in Tite Street. We have interviewed this man and he corroborates their statement. They returned here at three forty-five to find Madame Zoffany dead and the police in possession."

Sir Kit bent his head. "That is quite right," he said. "Agree, Victor?"

Soubise looked up with an effort. "Yes," he said dully.

"So between two and twenty-five past, as far as we can be certain," said Lee, "these two men were alone. Soubise admits he was in the house. Sir Christopher says he was in the garden. Neither of them admits seeing anyone else during that vital time."

"I saw no one, sir," said Kit stolidly.

"And you did not move from the greenhouse?"

"No."

"Very well." Lee appeared satisfied.

The tension in the room had become painful. Genevieve's black eyes moved to Margot's and held them.

"You see?" The words were not spoken, but the girl caught them as clearly as if they had been shouted. "You see? It will be as I said. A time comes when there is no one else. There are no miracles in these affairs."

Lee gave them no breathing space.

"So far," he pressed on, "I have not mentioned the motive. After all, no one commits an act like that, soaks a pad and forces it over the face of a poor old woman who so little expects it that she puts up no fight at all. No one does that unless he has a reason, you know. However, there are motives in this family. Most of you know all about them."

For the first time he appeared to hesitate, or rather to wait for something which did not come.

"I think we all know that Sir Christopher here had a motive for wanting his old friend out of the way and no more expense to him. Some might think it a very good motive," he announced loudly, while the superintendent winced.

But Kit did not explode. He shook his head gently. He said nothing, but the silent negation was very impressive. It was pitying, almost regretful.

Lee did not press it. His small eyes travelled to Felix, who huddled further down in his chair.

"Felix Monet had sufficient motive," said Lee, "or at least he evidently thought he had. He was so incensed against his employer that he smashed one of her most precious possessions and left his fingerprints all over it. Afterwards, when he remembered he had handled the chloroform bottle on discovering it, he jumped to the conclusion that the police, who were either mentally defective or dishonest, would link the crimes and convict him. He was so sure of this that he tried, not very hard, to hang himself."

"Monsieur——" Felix had struggled to his feet.

Lee waved him down, and the watchful Skinner completed the operation by jerking him back into his chair, where he subsided, his eyes bulging.

"Then there's Denis Cotton," said Lee. "Well, we've heard plenty about his motives and we won't go over them again. But he had them, all right, and so had Miss Robert, even if she was carefully out of the way during the actual moment of the attack."

He was speaking quietly and casually, but this time there was genuine speculation in his expression. The other two he had dismissed without real consideration, but now he was eager, and under the thin film of conversationalism the brisk voice had an edge.

"When my man surprised them in Dower Street they were in each other's arms," he said.

The protest came unexpectedly from Genevieve.

"If I could believe that, I could believe anything," she said spitefully. "Mademoiselle is affianced to Monsieur Victor."

Lee relaxed. He had had a long time to wait, but the ice was breaking now.

"I was told that," he said easily. "That provides more sources of strain, doesn't it? Makes us think, all us officials."

With a gesture he made them aware of the audience of policemen, whose faces remained blank apart from the irrepressible curiosity and excitement in their eyes.

"That gives Victor Soubise two motives," said Lee. "One against Madame Zoffany, one against Denis Cotton. But perhaps the particular difficulties experienced by Mr. Soubise are not so well known as they might be. It's true, isn't it, Mr. Soubise, that you lost your Brazilian fortune last year, and that you needed either Madame Zoffany's help or your inheritance from her estate? I haven't all the details yet, but the reports which have come to hand make it obvious to me that you had to get a very large sum of money very soon if you were going to save anything at all from the South American wreck. You were going to tackle Madame Zoffany about it this week end, weren't you? At any rate, that's what you told Messrs. Ribbon and Slater of London Wall yesterday."

Sir Kit made a curious little noise in his throat, and Margot turned to find him looking helplessly at Victor, now slowly straightening himself in his chair.

"I don't *know*, Sir Christopher," Lee said pointedly, "but I suggest Soubise told you some of his difficulties over lunch today."

"In confidence," said Kit stoutly.

"Of course, in confidence." The inspector was not exactly mimicking, but his tone was a smug repetition of Kit's own. "And then," he went on with huge satisfaction, "he left you for twenty minutes to go and have it out with the old lady. After that he came back and went for a walk with you, and when you both returned Madame Zoffany was dead and suspicion had fallen, mysteriously enough, on the man who had pinched his girl. How does that strike you?"

Kit's opinion, whatever it might have been, was never given. No one in the room was prepared for Victor's reaction. He sat stiffly in his chair, his eyes prominent, his face grey, and began to scream. No other description could fit the stream of denial which poured from his thin lips.

"Liar! Liar! It is not true. You are prevaricating. You are deceiving. I did not kill her. I did not kill her. Never! Never in my life. I did not see her. It is not true."

He was speaking in French and the rolling phrases were shouted at the top of his voice. The man was wild with terror. Fear started out of every pore. As an exhibition it was unnerving, and for the first time the inspector seemed in danger of losing his grip.

"What's he saying?" he demanded. "What is it, somebody? Quick!"

"*Menteur! Jamais!*" Victor was beginning again when Kit intervened.

"My dear fellow," he protested, the mild address contrasting vividly with the impassioned spate, "gently . . . Speak in a tongue the man understands. Take yourself in hand. Really, Soubise!"

The admonition had its effect. Victor subsided and began to speak more soberly.

"It is not true. I did not kill her."

"That is what I imagined you said." Lee was sardonic. "Anything to add?"

"Yes." Victor was sulky now and his lids were drawn down so low that only two narrow slits of his eyes remained.

"I did mean to tell Zoff about my difficulties, and on Kit's advice I did go up to see her, but I didn't go into the room because Denis was there."

"You listened at the door, I suppose?"

"Yes."

"Exactly." A contemptuous smile spread over the inspector's heavy face. "And then you came quietly away, I suppose, and went back to the garden? That it?"

"No." The thin lips made a circle on the word. "No, I went on up the stairs to my own room on the next floor."

"How long did you stay there?" Lee was frowning.

"About ten minutes, until I heard Denis come up to his room. I watched him through the crack of the door. He was carrying the green bag and he went into his own room to collect his suitcase. I saw him come out with it and go down again."

"One minute." Lee put up his hand and turned to Denis enquiringly. "You didn't tell me that."

"I'd forgotten it." Denis looked dazed. "It's true," he

said at last. "I'd forgotten. I did go up to get my own week-end case. That's right. I just looked in and picked it up before——"

"Wait." Lee turned back to Victor, who, though still trembling, was calmer and more coherent. "What happened then?"

"I crept out of my room and looked over the banisters, and I watched Denis go down to the hall."

"You what!" Lee roared, forgetting himself as his theory tottered. "You—— Oh, I see." He was smiling again. "Then you came down and opened the old lady's door and found her——"

"No." Victor could be contemptuous also. "No. I did not go in a second time either, because I heard her talking to someone."

The words dropped quietly into a pool of silence. Lee opened his mouth and closed it again without a sound, and the little echoes which Victor's statement made went reverberating gently round the room.

Oddly, it was the old superintendent, who hitherto had been perfectly quiet, who first took hold of the situation.

"To whom was she speaking, Mr. Soubise?"

"I don't know." Victor was hesitating, but his own bewilderment lent the words conviction. "I don't know. But it was someone she knew very well."

"How could you tell that?" Lee was back on the job again, mystified but intent and on the track like a hound.

"Because she said such an extraordinary thing. I didn't wait long because I heard Genevieve and Felix talking in the hall. They'd seen Denis go out with the bag and were discussing him. I listened to them for a bit while they chattered, but at last they went to the front door, presumably to look after him, and I saw my opportunity and slid down the stairs to the kitchen exit and hurried back to Sir Kit, who was where I had left him in the greenhouse."

His voice died away and Genevieve looked at Felix.

"That is so. We did not go up immediately."

"*Non.* Not for some few minutes. We went to the gate and watched Monsieur Denis disappear down the road. We were there quite a long time. I had forgotten."

"There seems to have been a lot of forgetting," Lee grumbled, but there was no suspicion in his voice. The two incidents were typical of the kind which in his experience were often forgotten by innocent people. Both were natural, ordinary movements, easily overlooked amid more sensational happenings.

He returned to Victor with savagery.

"You swear you heard Madame Zoffany talking to somebody she knew well, after you had seen Denis Cotton leave the house? You stick to that, even though you must realise that the statement puts you in an even more questionable position than you are in already?"

For a second it looked as though Victor were about to burst out again into another fit of hysterical denials, but he controlled himself.

"I am telling the truth," he said, moistening his dry lips. "I heard her distinctly."

"What was she saying?"

Victor hesitated. "It was so extraordinary," he said at last. "She was speaking so gently, but with such passion, if you understand. I only heard it through the door, but it was... it was pathetic and so quiet. She said—I heard her clearly—'*Tu penseras à moi quelquefois, n'est-ce pas? Et tu diras, "Eh bien, après tout, c'était une bonne fille..."*' That was all." His own voice softened on the words and took on a strange quality of regret.

"Oh my God!" It was Margot. The strangled words escaped her, and at the same moment Genevieve, her face a crumpled mask, stumbled to her feet.

"*Angelo!*" she said thickly.

Sir Kit raised his head, an expression of horrified recognition in his eyes.

"La Tisbe!" he whispered. "Victor, didn't you know?"

"Translate! Translate! Good heavens, what the hell is all this? Translate, someone, can't you?" Lee was beside himself, but the members of the household took no notice of him. They were looking at each other in frightened comprehension, and in the end it was the wretched Skinner, of all people, who came to the rescue.

"I was in France in the Army, sir," he mumbled, "and I picked up some of the lingo. I think what Mr. Soubise quoted means this, sir, roughly. 'You'—that's the familiar form of address, sir, only used in the family or among lovers, like; it's familiar—'you will think of me sometime, won't you? And you'll say, "Oh, well, after all, she was a good kid . . . "' That's about it, sir, something after that style."

Lee regarded his subordinate with grudging approval.

"Repeat that," he commanded.

Skinner obliged, growing even more roseate in the process.

"Is he right?" Lee appealed to Denis, who, with Victor, alone seemed unenlightened.

"Yes, I think so. A very fair translation. 'She was a good girl,' perhaps. But I still don't see what it conveys."

"Nor do I." The inspector made the words sound like an expletive. "Miss Robert, you cried out when you heard it. What does it mean to you? What do the words signify?"

She turned helplessly to Sir Kit.

"Oh, not me, Kit," she said simply. "I can't bear it."

"By the lord——" Lee was beginning when the old man took a step forward. He was obviously very shaken, but his voice was gentle and steady.

"Those words are a quotation from a play, Inspector. They occur at the end of the last act of Victor Hugo's tragedy of *Angelo*. It is not one of the great pieces, but many years ago Madame Zoffany scored a great personal success as the heroine and was always very fond of the part." He paused to take a deep breath while the whole room watched him in fascinated silence. "The passage comes," he went on slowly, "when the heroine

193

is dying after forcing her lover to kill her. After, in fact, she has committed suicide——"

"Suicide!" Lee pounced on the word and flung it back at him. "That woman never committed suicide. You all said yourselves it was the last thing she would consider."

"No." The little word crept out softly, and Margot stood looking at him directly, her vivid blue eyes wet with tears. "No," she repeated. "Don't you see, Inspector? Don't you all see what happened? *Zoff didn't mean to die.*"

Her statement melted into the silence. Lee was frowning, his round brown eyes peering out under puzzled brows.

"How do you make that?"

The girl swallowed painfully.

"It's the clause in the law of inheritance, Inspector," she said huskily. "If you'll reread it you'll see it's not only the heir who actually kills who is debarred from inheriting, but also the one who is convicted of attempting to kill. Zoff knew all about that, and I'm horribly afraid that she——" Her voice wavered and died, but she took hold of herself. "She had made two attempts to convince everyone that the heir she didn't like had tried to kill her, but no one had taken her seriously. On this last occasion I'm afraid she meant to make it very plain."

The young voice paused and then went on very steadily:

"This afternoon, the third time Zoff tried to convince us, she must have put too much chloroform on the towel. Gen'vieve was some time going up there, and when she found her, apparently dead, she replaced the cloth on her face."

## TEN

It took Inspector Lee some minutes to comprehend and afterward a much longer time to assemble the proofs and become convinced. But no one of Zoff's close associates doubted the truth after that first dazzling revelation. For them it was as if curtains had parted and swung upward in rustling festoons, to reveal Zoff's last tableau, the last scene in her final act.

From that moment it was she who dominated the drama of her death as completely as she had dominated all the many tragi-comedies which had made up her life. Once again she moved among them, as vital and compelling as ever, and her personality permeated the old house and coloured all their thoughts.

They were shocked and heartbroken but not mystified any longer. Zoff had sprung her last sensational surprise.

Lee had the play brought to him and the faded cuttings from the press book, flowery with praises for her interpretation of the part. The relevant passages were translated for him not only by Denis but also by Skinner, whose return to official favour was one of the minor miracles of the night.

Finally he sent for the Code Civil and read once more the important passage in the law governing inheritance, whose full significance he had not grasped that afternoon when the point had come up at the police station. The evidence was simple and irrefutable. When he had digested it he called them together again. He was still startled, but no longer on the chase, and the fire had gone out of him.

"I'll own I'm staggered," he said. "What an amazing woman!"

"She was amazing." Kit made it clear that he considered the description complimentary. "She was a great artist and a great woman. That was the explanation, Inspector. Above all, she was always feminine. That explains her. And," he added gently, "I think it excuses her. At least it does to me."

"Excuses?" Lee conveyed astonishment, but he had lost his anger and his protest was without violence. "She might have got young Cotton hanged."

"But she didn't mean to die." It was typical of their reaction that it was Denis himself who put forward the extenuating circumstance. Even in death Zoff was finding champions among those she had most ill-used.

Kit, who had seen it happen so many times in her life, recognized the phenomenon.

"No," he said. "Poor, poor girl, she didn't mean to die. And she didn't trust you with her real diamonds, either, Denis. That was a cruelly typical little touch. That ought to have told us." He turned to Lee. "She planned to be found unconscious, with poor Denis running away with her diamonds," he said, "but even so, she couldn't trust herself to part with the real ones. That was Zoff all over."

Lee gaped at him. "It was a deliberately engineered attempt to get Cotton disgraced, arrested and disinherited," he said. "I really don't see how you can find that forgivable."

They were silent until Margot sighed.

"You didn't know her," she said slowly. "If you'd only known her, Inspector, you'd have been furious with her but you'd have forgiven her. She wouldn't have let it happen quite like that, you see. She'd have done something else to make it all right."

Lee grunted. He was beginning to be profoundly relieved that he had not known the lady, but, glancing at the sorrowing faces around him, he forbore to say so. Instead, he raised a point which had been fascinating him.

"Did she always quote from her old plays when she got up to mis——I mean, whatever she was doing? Even when she was alone?"

"Madame was always acting, monsieur." Genevieve supplied the answer and made it clear that she felt she was recording a very fine and natural trait.

"They do, you know," put in Victor, speaking from his seat just outside the circle. "Old actors and actresses always quote all the time. They dramatise everything and often the words fit. I don't know why the explanation didn't occur to me at the time. If the words had not been so natural and so like her, I should have understood, but I didn't recognise them. She spoke with such sweet gentleness, and so simply, that I took it for granted she was talking to Kit, as a matter of fact." A flicker of embarrassment passed over his narrow face. "I imagined he had followed me up and gone in to her as Denis came out. When I got down to the greenhouse again and found him still there I could not possibly imagine who it was that had been with her. I was so miserable, and so bewildered, that I didn't care."

Nobody spoke and he settled back in his chair again, his long hands clasped over his knees. His forehead was still wet with sweat beads and his eyes were heavy.

Presently the police began to leave. In ten minutes they had changed from being enemies to very ordinary embarrassed officials, anxious to get home.

The superintendent and the sergeants melted out of the group and Lee prepared for departure. To Sir Kit his manner verged on the apologetic.

"I made a mistake," he said simply as they stepped aside for a moment. "I could see someone was being clever and I didn't pick on the right person." His glance wandered to Victor and rested there a moment. "I overestimated," he said. "Well, I must say, for everybody's sake I'm glad it turned out as it did."

"Are you, indeed?" The old man's quiet amazement was disconcerting.

Lee blinked and took refuge in being obliging.

"There'll be no need for the p.m. now," he murmured. "There'll be time to cancel it. I'll be seeing the press too. I promised them a statement tonight if they'd only leave me alone. They'll be waiting for me down at the Lion. You can rely on me to see it's put to them as decently as possible. As a matter of actual fact, it's an accident, I suppose. There'll be an inquest, of course, but—well, I shouldn't worry, sir."

He was behaving very handsomely and Kit recognised it.

"Very good of you," he said firmly. "I shall appreciate that, Inspector." To emphasise his gratitude he went down to the front door with him, beckoning first Margot and then Denis to follow. They all four shook hands on the step, and just before he went Lee hesitated and spoke to the girl.

"I hope I haven't upset your affairs, miss," he said, "but you can't—er—make omelettes without breaking eggs, you know."

As the door closed behind him Kit laughed softly.

"Queer fellow," he said. "Crude, clumsy, brutal in some ways, but embarrassingly well-meaning. Thank God he's gone. Now, if you two will come in here, there is something I must say to you tonight." He put his hands on their shoulders and steered them into the untidy drawing room. The fire had burnt to a heap of white wood ash, but he took up his position with his back to it and stood looking at them.

"I don't know if Margot should hear this," he began. "I've been wondering, but on the whole I think perhaps she should. Not for your sake, Denis, but for Zoff's. You may think," he went on, choosing his words with some difficulty, "that I think too much of Zoff. I do. I always have. She has been abominable. I wasn't going to admit it before that fellow, but this last act was wicked and it was unforgivably cruel. I loved her, I suppose, as much as any man has ever loved a woman, and I do most freely admit that she was often cruel, but you must let me tell you something in fairness to her."

"My dear Kit." Denis looked younger than his years in his sympathy and embarrassment. "Don't," he said gently. "It doesn't matter now. It's over. Let's forget——"

"No." The old man cut him short. "No," he repeated. "There's no forgetting, but there is understanding, and with that sometimes there comes forgiveness. She hated you, Denis, and I know why." He paused and looked at the girl. "Zoff was five years younger than you, Margot, when she married D'Hiver," he said. "He was twenty years older than she was, but she adored him. She was

a peasant and an actress, and he was the head of one of
the first families of France. His home was near her
own. She had known him and looked up to him from
babyhood. Before they married he made one extraordinary stipulation. He insisted that she should adopt and
bring up as her own the baby daughter who had just
been born to her own elder sister. This girl had died in
childbed, unmarried, and her disgrace was one of the
peasant family's chief annoyances at the time. D'Hiver
gave no explanations. He was like that. He commanded
and Zoff obeyed. The child was called Elise d'Hiver."

Denis was staring at him, deep furrows cutting his
forehead, his heavy chin thrust out.

"Then all that dreary old business of the court case
was justified," he said slowly.

"Hardly justified." Kit's lips grew crooked on the
word. "That case was one of Zoff's unforgivable cruel-
ties. Zoff had given her word to D'Hiver. She had her
portion of his fortune and the man was dead. She lost
her case and quite rightly. But her allegation was true.
Elise was not her own daughter. She was her sister's.
She never admitted that."

"Oh, but even so . . ." Margot was so sorry for him, so
anxious to spare him. "Even so, why should she hate
Denis?"

He looked from the one to the other of them unhappily.

"She hated Denis, my dear," he said, "because when
she saw him she saw D'Hiver. Felix recognised the
likeness. I saw it in his face the other day. I recognised
it. To Zoff it must have been a revelation. You are
D'Hiver, Denis, in modern clothes."

Denis passed his hand over his forehead.

"Then my mother," he said, "was——"

"Was D'Hiver's child but not Zoff's." Kit sat down.
"My dear boy," he said, "this is all fifty years ago."

"Zoff did not know it was his until she saw Denis?"

"Zoff was jealous," he agreed sadly. "Zoff never grew
old. That was her tragedy. Forgive her, Denis, if you
can. And now for God's sake don't try to do anything

199

quixotic about the money," he said briskly. "Most of it sprang from D'Hiver anyway. You're going to finance some sort of clinic, aren't you? Then do it. Let my poor girl have done a little bit of good."

He got up and went toward the door.

"I'm tired," he said pausing to look back at them. "There'll be a lot to do tomorrow. Don't come with me, my dears. I shall be all right."

Margot remained halfway toward him. His weariness was as vivid to her as if it had been her own. But there was one question she could not keep back.

"Kit," she said, "how did you know?"

He smiled at her. "I knew," he said, "because she left me for D'Hiver, long ago, when we were boy and girl. She loved him, not me, you see. Good night."

The door closed behind him but she remained looking at it until Denis went over and drew her down beside him. He put an arm around her and gathered her close to him.

"You're an actress too, and you suspected me of being a murderer," he said. "But I'm going to marry you. D'you know? If it's any comfort to you, there are no stipulations."

**THE END**

## ABOUT THE AUTHOR

MARGERY ALLINGHAM, who was born in London in 1904, came from a long line of writers. "I was brought up from babyhood in an atmosphere of ink and paper," she claimed. One ancestor wrote early nineteenth century melodramas, another wrote popular boys' school stories, and her grandfather was the proprietor of a religious newspaper. But it was her father, the author of serials for the popular weeklies, who gave her her earliest training as a writer. She began studying the craft at the age of seven and had published her first novel by the age of sixteen while still at boarding school. In 1927 she married Philip Youngman Carter, and the following year she produced the first of her Albert Campion detective stories, *The Crime at Black Dudley*. She and her husband lived a life "typical of the English countryside" she reported, with "horses, dogs, our garden and village activities" taking up leisure time. One wonders how much leisure time Margery Allingham, the author of more than thirty-three mystery novels in addition to short stories, serials and book reviews, managed to have.

# Murder Most British

With these new mystery titles, Bantam takes you to the scene of the crime. These masters of mystery follow in the tradition of the Great British crime writers. You'll meet all these talented sleuths as they get to the bottom of even the most baffling crimes.

# THE THRILLING AND MASTERFUL NOVELS OF ROSS MACDONALD

Winner of the Mystery Writers of America Grand Master Award, Ross Macdonald is acknowledged around the world as one of the greatest mystery writers of our time. *The New York Times* has called his books featuring private investigator Lew Archer "the finest series of detective novels ever written by an American."

Now, Bantam Books is reissuing Macdonald's finest work in handsome new paperback editions. Look for these books (a new title will be published every month) wherever paperbacks are sold or use the handy coupon below for ordering:

☐ SLEEPING BEAUTY (24593 * $2.95)

☐ THE MOVING TARGET (24546 * $2.95)

☐ THE GOODBYE LOOK (24192 * $2.95)

☐ THE NAME IS ARCHER (23650 * $2.95)

☐ THE BLUE HAMMER (24497 * $2.95)

☐ BARBAROUS COAST (24268 * $2.95)

☐ BLUE CITY (22590 * $2.95)

☐ INSTANT ENEMY (24738 * $2.95)

**Prices and availability subject to change without notice.**